MICKEY OUTSIDE

Text copyright © 2014 by David T. Lender
All rights reserved.
Printed in the United States of America.

Published by Thomas & Mercer
P.O. Box 400818
Las Vegas, NV 89140

ISBN-13: 9781477848968
ISBN-10: 1477848967
Library of Congress Control Number: 2013910735

MICKEY OUTSIDE

A WHITE COLLAR CRIME THRILLER BY

DAVID LENDER

THOMAS & MERCER

For Cindy Begin

ALSO BY DAVID LENDER

Sasha Del Mira Series
Trojan Horse
"Sasha Returns" (A Short Story)
Arab Summer

Other Thrillers
The Gravy Train
Bull Street
Vaccine Nation
"Rudiger" (A Short Story)

ACKNOWLEDGMENTS

Thank you to Cindy Begin for being my first draft reader and critic, and to Manette for your comments and for your love and support throughout the process.

Thank you to David Downing for another great editing job. Your suggestions and comments were indispensable. You're a pleasure to work with.

And thank you again to the team at Amazon Publishing.

CHAPTER 1

Mickey Steinberg sat at a picnic table, watching a softball game on the diamond at the Federal Prison Camp, Yankton, South Dakota, the unfenced minimum-security prison he'd called home for two years and ten months. It was the first game of the FPC Yankton World Series, and the bleachers were filled with a noisy crowd of over 200 inmates and their visitors. The smells of hot dogs and freshly cut grass were in the air. Mickey enjoyed the sun on his face and arms, but if he closed his eyes he could still see the scene in the South Dakota winter, the lush grass a forbidding expanse of rock-hard tundra, the warm breeze a subzero wind that sliced like razors.

Mickey was chatting with the guard they called Sly, who stood next to him. The man had once confided to Mickey that he knew why the inmates nicknamed him Sly: he was built like a young Sylvester Stallone and could bench press 390 pounds. Mickey never told him it was really because Sly was as dumb as Rocky in the movie. Mickey was patient with him, though, explained things to him when no one else was around, so Sly wouldn't feel as if he was as dumb as he was. Mickey had also been struggling to tutor him through his GED high school equivalency for two years.

Mickey had just commented to Sly that if somebody clobbered one to straightaway center, the inmate playing center field could follow the ball into the trees and keep going straight across Douglas Avenue, like the only inmate to have ever escaped had done seven years ago.

When the batter yanked one down the left-field line, Mickey saw Sly's body tense as the left fielder chased it down toward the Forbes Building. The left fielder, Steve Gleason, a man in his late 50s, in for seven years for embezzling $2.6 million from Canton Savings Bank, caught the ball in foul territory. Gleason then lumbered toward Douglas Avenue before he circled back and threw the ball in. Mickey couldn't tell if Gleason was jerking the guards' chains or hot-dogging for the fans.

"So you were sayin'," Sly said, "you're lookin' for a certain type."

"Picture a BMW car salesman. Good-looking, well-dressed, well-spoken, but with an edge, so he doesn't come off as too smooth, but maybe as a little slick, even dangerous."

"You want him for pickin' up chicks?"

"No. But think about it, you have to admit that type appeals to you and can sell you."

"You sayin' you think I'm gay?"

Mickey restrained a sigh. "Of course not. I'm saying even men identify with that type. Men who watch James Bond movies, for example. Think image advertising. The Marlboro Man."

"Marlboros are bland. Camels are a real cigarette."

"You're missing the point. Marlboro picked that image because you identify with the Marlboro Man—"

"I just told you—"

"—alright, *people* identify with the Marlboro Man. That's why they buy the cigarette. That's what I'm looking for."

"Somebody like the Marlboro Man?"

"No, a man who fits a different type, the BMW salesman."

"What for?"

"Somebody I can get to know in here, hook up with for when we both get out. For a deal to get me started again."

"Started again? A big-time Wall Streeter like you? You must be loaded, have a pile waiting for you when you get out."

"I wish." Mickey reached down and turned his pockets inside out. Between what the Feds took from him in fines, his legal expenses, and with Rachel hacking off half his assets with the divorce, right now he had about $3,500 in the bank. Add to that the additional few hundred he'd make each month teaching accounting, basic finance and GED courses for the other inmates and guards. That, and whatever he could convince Rachel to loan him for a fresh start after he got out.

Sly said, "Then you really need this guy and this deal, huh? A man's nothin' if he's gotta settle for bein' a has-been nobody the rest of his life."

Mickey nodded.

"So what's in it for me?"

Mickey raised his eyebrows. "Haven't I gone out of my way to help you on your GED? You've said yourself it will raise you two pay grades after you get it."

"Yeah, but this won't be easy. There's like, eight hunnert guys in here."

"Yes. Hard to get to know them all. That's why I need your help."

"I can't just walk in, pick and choose who I get reassigned."

Mickey remained silent. *Here we go.*

Sly said, "I'll need you to sign off on my GED."

"You're only halfway through. I can't do that."

Sly didn't answer right away, then asked, "Then how can you expect my help?"

Mickey let it hang a moment. Sly was dumb, but he had street smarts. Mickey figured it would turn out this way; that's how he would have played it himself. "Okay, deal. You find me my type, I'll sign your papers." Mickey stood, gave him a big smile and slapped him on the back.

Sly leaned away and squinted at him.

Mickey said to himself, *You see?* He knew from long experience that he couldn't carry off the hail-fellow-well-met routine. He needed a talker, a salesman. Somebody born to it, who was just smart enough to understand what Mickey laid out for him to do, and polished enough to sell it. Somebody who could walk into a room at a conference, any conference, and come away with 50 business cards from people to pitch later. The type of man, like Sly had said, who could pick up women. A man who was shameless and wouldn't take no for an answer.

Somebody like Jack Grass, his former partner at Walker & Company, the investment bank they ran together for almost 20 years. Jack, the charismatic salesman who roped in the clients with impetuous promises. Promises that Mickey, the quiet one with the brains, figured out how to make into deals with his genius at financial engineering and his insight into human nature. A team that did their ham-and-egg magic until Mickey dreamed up the idea to start buying the stock of their clients' takeover targets in secret offshore accounts, based on inside information before the deals were made public. An idea he now wished his talker had talked him out of.

After they got caught, Jack turned on Mickey, so Mickey did him one better and cut a deal before Jack could. He told the Feds everything as part of a plea bargain for a short sentence in a white-collar prison. The Feds stuck to their word. They put him in Yankton, one of the cushiest country clubs in the Federal Bureau of Prisons. The place had everything—plenty of computers with e-mail in the study rooms, a weekly bookmobile, pool tables, Ping-Pong, music lessons, intramural sports, a huge gym, a track, vocational training and stress reduction classes—everything except tennis courts and a golf course.

Now that Mickey's roommate had just been released, he saw a perfect opportunity to find a new partner—another talker—to help in his resurrection. Mickey knew Sly would come through: he didn't stand a chance of passing his GED unless Mickey signed for him. And Mickey was scheduled for release in two months.

Paul Reece walked with the guard, Sly, beside the Forbes Building, the Romanesque redbrick building that was the former main building for Yankton College before the Feds turned it into a prison camp in the 1980s. Sly had walked into Paul's room five minutes earlier and told him Mickey Steinberg, the man himself, wanted to meet him. They now stepped out of the lush grass next to the baseball diamond, then crossed a stretch of dusty earth with tufts of unwatered grass toward where Mickey sat alone on one of those built-in benches to a picnic table, his newspaper spread out on the top.

A week in, Paul was still out of his element, uncertain. He always relied on a smile, a can-do attitude and his firm handshake to break the ice. But here in Yankton he had no idea how it worked, how he needed to conduct himself to get an introduction started in the right direction.

As they approached, Paul could see Mickey wasn't much to look at. A little paunchy and soft, not very tall, with frizzy Jewish hair. Mickey didn't glance up until they stopped beside the table, then showing lazy, blinking eyes.

Sly said, "This here's Paul Reece, the guy I told you about, another Wall Streeter. He arrived last week. He's in unit two over at Kingsbury right now, but we could move him into Lloyd with you if you guys get along."

"Don't get up," Paul said, and stepped forward to shake Mickey's hand, pumping it hard. "Nice to meet you."

"You too," Mickey said. His gaze went from Paul to Sly. He nodded and Sly moved off.

Paul sat down, reminding himself that Mickey was regarded as one of the smartest guys on Wall Street, and for whatever reason Mickey had summoned him, that this was a rare opportunity. *Don't blow this.*

Mickey took in Paul, watching him sit down after that forceful handshake, imagining what he'd look like in a suit, all 6'3" of him, almost as solid as Sly, in his mid-30s, hazel eyes without a hint of world-weariness, eager. He wore a friendly smile.

Mickey thought he looked the part. But so did the five others Sly had brought him, all duds. *Let's see if this one can talk.*

Mickey saw Paul's gaze go up over his shoulder as he felt someone put a hand on his back. Mickey turned. It was Stanley Cohn, an accountant from Cleveland, in for eight years for misdirecting $600,000 of clients' IRS refunds on e-filed tax returns to his personal bank account.

He had two men in tow.

"Mind if we sit down?" Cohn asked.

Mickey didn't respond.

Cohn was a dope, always trying to ingratiate himself with Mickey, introducing new inmates to him because Mickey was a celebrity around there. Cohn sat down next to Mickey, the two other men on the bench across from Cohn and next to Paul.

"This is Randy Sturgis and Jim Weiss, new around here." Cohn never looked at Paul or made any move to introduce the men to him.

Mickey nodded.

"Fellas, I'm sure you know who Mickey is—everybody does—on account of the $2 billion in profits his insider trading ring racked up over all those years, and him having Harold Milner, who I'm sure you also know on account of his being takeover maven of his generation, as Mickey's top client, at the center of it all."

Mickey looked Cohn in the eye. The last time Cohn did this he referred to Mickey as "Ivan Boesky and Mike Milken to the 10th power," after which Mickey sent Cohn's neck receding into his shoulders with a glare.

There was an awkward pause as Mickey and Cohn looked at each other for a long moment, Mickey now sure Cohn remembered the last time, too. Mickey turned his gaze to the two men and said, "Welcome to Club Fed."

As Mickey was turning to introduce Paul, Cohn said, "Fellas, I told you Mickey was an expert on deals, that maybe he can give you some advice on the Brinker and Sterling deal."

Mickey tensed. *Not this nonsense again.* "I've been out of the mainstream for over two years."

The man introduced as Sturgis cleared his throat and said, "I had a position in Sterling's stock prior to Brinker's takeover offer and I'm wondering should I hang on for a higher offer or take my profit and run?"

"I don't know anything about the deal," Mickey said. He turned to Paul again. "This is Paul Reece, also new in here, a fellow Wall Streeter. Maybe he has some perspective."

Paul opened his mouth to speak.

Cohn cut him off, saying, "That's okay," still not even looking at Paul. "We'd like your opinion, Mickey."

"Let the man talk."

Paul's face brightened, as if the teacher had called on him. He said, "It's an all-cash bid, so it stands by itself. Simple."

Sturgis said, "Yes, but Sterling's board of directors has rejected the offer."

Paul said, "Right, they always do that first. So either somebody else steps in and offers more, or Sterling's board squeezes Brinker for a higher offer."

"But what if Brinker won't offer more?"

Paul smiled. "Not possible. You ever take your best shot out of the box when, say, you're trying to buy a house or a car?" Paul continued, now getting loose, his voice confident, starting to gesture as if he were addressing clients at a dinner. "Brinker's CEO isn't gonna surface a public offer for Sterling to suffer the embarrassment of limping away with no deal."

Mickey was starting to enjoy himself.

Cohn said, "Do you know Brinker's CEO?" making it sound like an accusation.

Paul went right back at him. "No, but I'm talking about common sense. If Sterling's board said no, Brinker's CEO isn't just gonna say, 'Okay,' and walk away without at least bumping his bid higher."

Mickey said, "I know John Dobbs, the CEO of Brinker. He's an egomaniac."

Paul said, "There you go—but it doesn't matter if he is or not." He looked back at Sturgis. "If you sell your stock now, you're betting against human nature. Dobbs'll go higher."

Mickey added, "Even if Sterling is already fully valued," unable to resist a little ham-and-egg to top it off.

Cohn said to Paul, "What was your position on Wall Street?"

"I was a stockbroker."

Cohn wrinkled his nose. "I'd still feel better if you gave us your opinion, Mickey."

Mickey felt a twist of annoyance. "Don't be so quick to judge," he said to Cohn. "When I was on the Street, my deals involved a big network of contacts, really smart people, many of whom never came to light. You never know where one of them might surface." He looked over at Paul, then made eye contact with Cohn again.

Sturgis stood up, said, "Thanks for your time, guys." He narrowed his eyes at Cohn and said, "Come on, Stan, we've imposed on Mickey enough. Let's go."

After Cohn and the two men with him got up and walked off, Paul said to Mickey, "Why'd you infer that I was part of your ring?" He looked pained.

"Imply."

Paul looked at him as if he was confused.

"Never mind," Mickey said.

"No offense, but I've never traded on insider information and I don't like the idea of anybody thinking I have."

"If they do believe you were part of my 'ring,' as you call it, you just went up about 10 notches in their esteem. In here there's a social hierarchy. If you've got status, you don't need to worry about some slippery little worm like Cohn snitching on you if, for example, Sly sneaks you in a bottle of Bordeaux once a week, like he does for me. Relax, I just did you a favor."

———◇———

Paul figured that was good advice. After that they talked, hunched over the table on opposite sides. Paul telling Mickey stories, figuring this was kind of a job interview.

Paul telling Mickey that he got recruited from his high school in Hawley, PA, for a full ride at USC to play tight end, then getting cut from the football team in his sophomore year, switching from a physical education major to business. Telling him about dropping out due to lack of interest and grades reflecting it in his last semester of that year, then looking around for something to do, working stunts in films for a while, tending bar a few years, modeling, mostly for underwear ads, finally enrolling in the LA police academy, graduating and then paying his dues in the LAPD, working his way up.

Telling him about how he shot a guy once when he was a cop. Standing on the second-floor porch outside a house full of perps on a drug bust, looking in the window with his gun drawn, then hearing shooting start and seeing a guy's head inside the window not three feet away, and—pop—shooting him, then seeing another perp pointing a shotgun at him and ducking back just as the perp blows out the window. Telling Mickey about him tumbling backward down the steps, fracturing his T11 and T12 vertebrae. Not only that, him getting addicted to OxyContin painkillers while he's recovering.

Telling him when he gets out of the hospital his wife's dressing like a biker, cutting her hair short and getting tattoos. Then when he's in rehab to get off the Oxy, his wife going to the other side, taking up with Joni, her therapist.

"Last I heard they were adopting a kid. I tell you, man, some seriously bizarre shit happens in California. Give me New York, Wall Street any day." He gave Mickey a big smile like they were old pals. Then he squinted to show he was in earnest as he started his story again. "They put me on disability, unfit for cop work anymore, so I decided to get out of LA. The markets were red-hot when I came to New York and took my Series 7 exam, became a stockbroker. Went to some rinky-dink investment bank, Belcher Securities, with about 50 brokers selling the bejesus out of penny stock IPOs."

"A bucket shop."

"Yeah. Most of the guys snorting blow every day, and me just out of rehab, it was hard. But selling those crappy stocks to our clients, that was even harder."

"You do okay?"

Paul grinned. "I'm here, aren't I?"

Mickey showed a trace of a smile, his head nodding a little, his eyes with that lazy blink.

Paul leaned in farther and went on. "Yeah, I made good money. When we weren't pumping out a new deal every week, we were selling anything we could get our hands on that the other firms were taking public. I was on a roll for a few years. I had an apartment in Tribeca, wore a different custom suit every day, had models on my arm and drove a Porsche 911 Turbo. Then our clients started complaining that the stocks we were selling them were dropping like stones—most of the companies were technology startups and never got off the ground. When the SEC and the U.S. Attorney's Office stepped in, everybody ran for the exits."

"Except you."

"I was smart enough to know there was no place to run. Plus, I was only a cog in the wheel, not one of the guys turning the crank. That's what I told the Feds and they believed me."

"You mean you copped a plea and turned everybody else in."

Paul grinned, impressed. *Man, this guy's a quick study.* "Bet your ass. The Feds gave me a good deal. Not too bad a fine—$100,000—and six months in a country club."

Paul saw Mickey nod and gaze off in the distance like he was thinking, then smile.

After he left Mickey, Paul took stock of his situation. What did he have? What was he gonna do when he got out of Yankton? He'd scraped and clawed his way out of the Belcher Securities situation, danced with the Feds to cut a deal. He got out of it with barely his skin and not much else.

At least he'd kept himself in the game with Jennifer. He'd managed to get arrested, cop a plea and get sentenced without losing her, all by telling the truth—at least pretty much. If he had nothing else left, he figured Jennifer was enough for him. Enough for any man. There was a certain advantage to being with a woman who was smarter than him: it took away all that wasted energy of trying to think around her to get away with stuff he knew would piss her off anyhow. It made for a calmer existence, one where he could see a long-term future with her.

And he didn't have much else left, except maybe Sean and Carolyn, his big sister Marlene's kids. When he was with them he felt the flesh-and-blood connection. He'd seen lots of Sean and Carolyn when he lived in LA, doing his best to be a role model.

He took them to parks and zoos, would've even taken them fishing, which bored him to death, if there'd been any place to do it in the LA area.

With Marlene as a mother who couldn't get off the drugs, and a father who'd been run off by that fact, the kids needed all Uncle Paul could give them. There was nobody else. Paul's mom and dad were off on another of their perpetual missions, this one to someplace in Africa. Dad, the much holier one, in charge because of his greater righteousness. Mom, ever the follower who kept her mouth shut. Dad's way of helping Marlene's situation was to say to her, "Jesus forgives you—whether you're a drug addict, a child beater, a prostitute, whatever—he forgives you, with no judgment of your actions, no matter what." So Marlene, who bought into the party line that Dad dictated, woke up every morning with a fresh slate, forgiven, and got right back to it all over again.

Early in his life Paul realized it was Dad who handled the judgment department, always with his stern disapproval, no matter what. Well man, Paul made up his mind a long time ago he was no longer seeking Dad's approval, or forgiveness.

After Paul came to New York and was riding high on Wall Street, he made sure to fly back to LA once every few months to do what he could for his nephew and niece. Once when Marlene asked him, he brought $5,000 in cash for Sean's braces. After Paul gave the money directly to the orthodontist, Paul had to tell Marlene that Jesus really wanted Sean to have those braces to make sure Marlene wouldn't try to get her hands on the five grand to spend it on something else.

So as Paul considered his situation, he had an open mind to whatever Mickey might propose.

After hearing Paul spew stories, Mickey was convinced Paul had potential. *But will he play along?* The next day he searched the Internet for *Paul Reece* on one of the computers in the unit study room. The kid's story basically checked out. He showed up with a marriage announcement to Mary Agnes Begin, a computer programmer from Salinas, California, ten years earlier, then as a hero policeman in the LAPD, injured in action in a drug bust four years after that. His divorce papers a year later were public record, too.

Then nothing for a stretch, then his plea bargain when the Feds brought down Belcher Securities earlier that year. Paul had left some facts out of that story as he'd told it to Mickey. He wasn't a mere cog in the machinery: he'd confessed to being fully engaged in the firm's Internet spam campaign, exaggerated press releases and telemarketing tactics through Belcher Securities' brokers in executing its "pump and dump" strategy. The firm induced investors to buy penny stocks that Belcher had taken huge positions in, then sold them once the unwitting investors had run up their prices, leaving the investors holding the bag. Paul had cut himself a great deal because he'd been able to lay out the scheme for the Feds down to the last detail.

That answered Mickey's question as to whether or not Paul would play along.

Now he realized he needed to get serious about the money, a stake to get him started again.

Felons convicted of insider trading weren't good risks for loan officers at any of the banks he knew, and his friends on Wall Street weren't about to take his calls. That left Rachel.

Rachel had filed for divorce a month after Mickey was indicted. In retrospect, it wasn't hard for him to understand her position.

"I feel as if I don't know you," she'd said after he'd explained that everything in his indictment was true. She'd then asked, "Has this whole thing been a sham, too?"

"What whole thing?"

"Our marriage."

It had cut him so deeply that he'd been unable to respond. Then he realized that for her to even have asked the question meant his betrayal of her trust had cut her even deeper. The next day he moved out of their apartment and into the Waldorf until his trial.

He'd never planned on going to jail, but now seeing how badly he'd hurt Rachel, he realized it would be naïve to have any romantic illusions about his woman waiting for him until he got out. Besides, Rachel had her charities and wealthy girlfriends, the wives of his colleagues on Wall Street and the big law firms and banks he did business with, all of whom shunned him like he was radioactive after he was indicted. Rachel and he were a mature couple in their 50s, not some young lovers, and the glue of the marriage by that time in their lives was their social circle, particularly since they didn't have children. It was only natural to Mickey that Rachel would want to continue that life when he became unstuck from it.

The night before she filed divorce papers she called him. Her voice was faint, wooden.

"I've hired a lawyer. He says my only logical course of action is to stake my claim on half our marital assets, so the courts can only take your half in fines after you're convicted. I'm sorry, Mickey. I . . ." Her voice trailed off.

"I understand," was all Mickey said before he hung up, his head feeling like his skull was being crushed.

Rachel was still living in their—now her—Park Avenue co-op.

It was a far cry from their first apartment in New York, a 1,200-square-foot duplex condominium on 32nd Street between Lex and Third that they really couldn't afford, but which Rachel pushed Mickey to stretch for.

"We won't have much money left after the mortgage payment. We'll be sitting on cardboard boxes for years," Mickey had said.

"Doesn't your bank give an employee discount that will save us points on the mortgage?"

Mickey had to hand it to her. For someone who might never have balanced her checkbook, Rachel knew how to speak to Mickey in his own language. Looking for another way out, Mickey turned to face the spiral staircase to the second floor. "I'll probably smash my kneecaps every time I run downstairs to answer the door for takeout."

"I'll learn to cook," was Rachel's response.

They bought the place. Mickey was wrong about the cardboard boxes: Rachel furnished it over six months with a willing salesman, Steven Schwartz, of B. Altman & Co., the department store on 34th Street and Fifth Avenue. Steven took her list of desired items and kept an eye out for display models, close-out deals and sales.

Mickey got used to picking up the phone to: "Hi, Mickey, it's Steven. Please tell Rachel I found another one on her list."

Mickey and Rachel had met at temple in Elizabeth, New Jersey, when they were both in grammar school. Mickey's father, Saul, was accountant to Rachel's father, Marvin Feldman, a bagel mogul with six Mr. Bagel retail locations in Elizabeth, Newark, Jersey City and Hoboken. Mr. Feldman was a big man in Elizabeth, and an authority figure around the temple who always stepped up with a flourish to finance the gap in the temple's budget for new construction projects.

Mickey saw his father as always in Mr. Feldman's shadow, part of the reason Mickey decided he wanted to be more than some dreary accountant who huddled in the background. It took Mickey until his 20s to appreciate how instrumental his father had been behind the scenes at the temple, even devising the life insurance scheme that would perpetuate funding it. The congregation collectively took out a $10 million life insurance policy on one of its younger members every five years or so, locking in low premiums for whole life policies that the temple could borrow against in emergencies, and finance its long-term future as its members eventually passed away. He thought it was amusing that one such policy had been taken out on him, and imagined that today the congregation's members wished him dead for more than one reason.

Rachel was the dweeby little kid, three years younger than Mickey, who sat with her family four rows in front of his every Saturday. He saw Rachel every week at temple through high school, then only on and off during summers after they both went off to college—he to Brown on a combination of academic scholarships and student loans, she to Amherst on the wings of her father's bagel empire.

By the time he encountered her again in New York City, she was an assistant editor at Macmillan, he a 30-year-old rising vice president in commercial lending at Manufacturers Hanover Bank, already making more than his father. The dweeby kid had grown into her nose and abandoned her glasses for contact lenses that unleashed penetrating brown eyes, framed by wavy brunette hair. She had the lithe body of a woman who played squash three times a week, even though she didn't, and was strong-willed enough to declare to her father that she no longer ate carbohydrates—including bagels—not only for the sake of her figure, but also her health.

Marvin Feldman let that slide, but was vocal about Mickey: "You should be with a man with a true background, a solid family."

When Mickey heard that he told Rachel, "You'd think he'd be happy you're not still with that WASP from Amherst who wore pink sweaters and plaid pants."

Rachel's response to Feldman had been, "Mickey went to Brown, Daddy."

"Anybody can get lucky and cobble together some loans and scholarships," Feldman said.

"He's a VP at a major New York bank with men your age reporting to him."

"It's a bank. Anybody with a pulse is a VP."

"I love him."

"Love is easy. Life is hard."

"Stop it, Daddy. He makes me happy."

To Mickey, Feldman said things like, "There's a world of difference between being an employee and an entrepreneur. Working for a bank you'll never have to worry about meeting a payroll or getting stuck with $20,000 of product on a truck that's broken down on the Pulaski Skyway."

Mickey would always smile, quietly despising the man. More than once Mickey spoke a silent "You see?" to Feldman in his mind after putting in the extra hour or rethinking a deal five more times, making something work that was unworkable just to show the old bastard.

But whatever Feldman thought of him, Mickey knew his ultimate revenge was that he'd won Rachel. She was his prize. At their wedding, Feldman had seemed triumphant as he'd presided over the extravagant reception at the Short Hills Country Club, but Mickey could see the defeat in his eyes as he'd shaken hands and welcomed Mickey into the family.

Four years into their marriage Rachel began to wonder why she hadn't conceived, and learned from a series of doctors that she was barren. She was in her mid-30s and the fact flipped some switch in her brain. Mickey worried about her over the next few months when she refused to talk about it, or even discuss adopting a child, and pushed herself harder into her career. The next few months turned into the next few years until she became the youngest editor ever at Macmillan. Afterward she told Mickey she realized she'd been depressed. Mickey found her a therapist and she made the regular trek up to 92nd and Broadway to Dr. Stein's office for two years. Then she abruptly stopped seeing Dr. Stein, gave up her job and started smoking. Almost overnight she became one of New York's prominent faces in the Jewish charity scene.

By then Mickey was running the Mergers and Acquisitions Group at Walker & Company, making millions as Jack Grass' partner.

After an article in the *Wall Street Journal* cited Mickey as one of the highest paid young stars on Wall Street, Rachel said, "I think you may have finally managed to shut Daddy up."

He'd have to be struck dumb by a stroke, Mickey thought.

It took another five years for a heart attack to do it.

Mickey figured that Feldman losing his fortune when he turned the business over to Rachel's idiot brother, Stanley, contributed to his death. Immediately after he'd taken over, Stanley had opened five locations in Manhattan, sparking what the *New York Post* called the "Great Bagel War" with B&B Bagels, the reigning New York bagel king, and driving Feldman's business into bankruptcy within nine months. After Feldman's death, Mickey waited for Rachel to finish grieving, then when she didn't after a few years, he realized the size of the hole Feldman's death left in her life. Then she found the Park Avenue apartment and threw herself into renovating and redecorating it. Mickey was happy about the apartment because the process seemed to fill up that hole, level Rachel out. She kept at it for years, Mickey blithely throwing money at it.

Now it was hers. And so was half the $20 million he was worth—after disgorgement of his share of the insider trading gains—that she got in the divorce before the Feds could grab it. He figured she'd be good for whatever he needed.

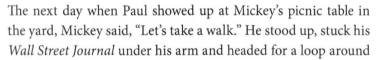

The next day when Paul showed up at Mickey's picnic table in the yard, Mickey said, "Let's take a walk." He stood up, stuck his *Wall Street Journal* under his arm and headed for a loop around the baseball field.

Paul started talking before they reached the thick grass alongside the first-base line.

"I've been thinking about it. What I don't understand is why a smart guy like you did what you did. I mean, I realize, man, if you're gonna cheat, cheat big. But you had everything going for you, at the top of your game. Great reputation. Must've been making scads of money. Probably owned a big chunk of Walker & Company. And Walker was one of the hottest firms on the Street. Why'd you do it, and how'd you let yourself get caught?"

"Most scams go unnoticed when they're small, then stick out like crazy when they get big. People get greedy. That's when they get caught. My case was no different. Harold Milner was our biggest client, doing a major takeover deal every 18 months or so. About six years ago he started getting pissed off because leaks on the Street about his deals were causing people to front run his bids—buying up the target stock before his offer. They'd run up the price and make his deals more expensive. It drove him crazy. That gave me an idea. If we could just piggyback a little on what other people were doing, no one would notice. On the first two deals we did it, we made almost as much money front running him as we did in fees for the deals. So I said to myself, 'We've got a great new business here.' We decided to ramp up the scale. We found two big foreign institutions with worldwide networks of operations to put $250 million into Walker & Company for a big minority stake. Then we used their capital to expand the side business into Walker's biggest profit center. It went great for about four years.

"Then some young MBA we hired stumbled by accident on one of the computer accounts we used to send out our orders to buy the stock of Milner's—and others'—takeover targets. The kid got curious and started following what was happening.

"Around that time the SEC created this new MarketWatch computer program, which could track orders to buy the stock of any company from anyplace around the world. They got wise, put in wiretaps and even sicced computer hackers on it. They traced it back to the kid, thinking he was involved. When the SEC and U.S. Attorney's Office sweated the kid, he went directly to Milner to try to figure a way out of it. Milner had been in on it for the last few years, because he found out we were part of the front running, got pissed off and made us pay him back $200 million, his estimate of what our side business had cost him in inflated prices for his takeover targets. We cut him into the deal to pay him back, so he was dirty, too.

"He and the kid teamed up and scammed the foreign partners by blackmailing them. They threatened to go to the Feds with what they knew unless they paid them off. The foreign partners agreed. Milner and the kid took everything they knew to the Feds and cut a deal to save their asses.

"To make matters worse, as the thing was unraveling, my partner, Jack Grass, hired some of his old buddies from Canarsie in Brooklyn to kill two people who were ready to turn evidence over to the Feds—Milner's CFO and Walker's General Counsel— and tried to have the kid and Milner hit, too."

Paul said, "Why didn't you go to the Feds yourself, cut a deal when you found out what Jack was doing?"

"I tried. I was negotiating a deal through my lawyer, but Milner beat me to it. Milner's deal broke everything open. My lawyer's advice was to wait until after Jack and I were arraigned, see what they were throwing at me before deciding what to do. Before I could do anything, Jack sent his Canarsie friends after me to shut me up in case I was going to talk. One of them took a shot at me and missed."

"Man, some partner."

"At that point I figured it was every man for himself. I told the Feds everything I knew, including about the murders by Jack and the Canarsie boys in exchange for three years out here."

Paul said, "So it didn't turn out so bad, huh?"

"Not so bad if you consider that my fines and my divorce took every nickel I had, I lost my securities licenses and I'm banned from the business for life." They were deep in center field now, the trees 20 yards away, Davidson Avenue just beyond them. Mickey was thinking about a line he thought might be from a song, *If a man's got nothing, he's got nothing to lose.*

Paul said, "Sorry to hear that. I think I might be able to get my licenses back eventually."

"It wouldn't be worth it. Nobody on the Street would hire you."

Paul paused for a moment, then said, "So what's next for you?"

"Maybe that's where you come in. Some kind of deal after we get out. I'm not sure what yet. But if we're going to make any real money, it won't be legal." Mickey waited for Paul to respond. When he didn't, Mickey said, "I guess with you being a former law-enforcement officer, maybe that's not very appealing to you."

"You're forgetting that I'm no longer fit for cop work."

Mickey turned to Paul and smiled. He'd found his talker. Now he needed to find his deal.

A month later, Mickey was primed for release. Paul and Mickey were already a team. Paul was on board for whatever deal Mickey dreamed up, and he'd be out in a maximum of four months after Mickey, less if he got time off for good behavior.

It was noon when Mickey walked to the unit study room. A half-dozen inmates were using the computers; another few talked on the phones. He found an unoccupied phone, entered his access code and dialed Rachel's phone number at the apartment. Rachel picked up on the first ring, her voice gravelly. "Hello?"

"Rachel, hi, it's Mickey."

She cleared her throat. "Are you out yet?"

"In a month. I thought you were going to quit smoking."

She paused, then said in a lowered voice, "It's a hard habit to break."

"I guess so. Listen, I could use your help."

"I'll do anything I can, within reason, you know that, Mickey."

"I'm going to need some capital to get a fresh start."

Rachel didn't respond.

"You wound up with all of our money. I could use a loan."

"How much are you talking about?"

"A million dollars."

"Mickey, you've got to be kidding me."

"You know I'm good for it."

"I don't have that kind of cash."

"Of course not, but when we did our settlement, among other things you got $8 million in money market funds, stocks and bonds. They're all liquid. You can just sell something."

"I don't have it. And even if I did . . ." She cleared her throat. "Even if I did, Walter would never agree to it."

Mickey's stomach muscles tensed. "Walter? Walter who?"

"Walter Goldstein. You know who he is."

"Walter Goldstein, the art dealer?" Of course Mickey knew him. A slick-talking, pompous boob who flitted around charity functions and tried to impress the ladies with his mellifluous baritone.

"Yes."

"What's he got to do with it?"

"He's my fiancé."

Mickey felt it like a smack in the forehead. "You're going to *marry* the man? *That* man?"

Rachel went on. "Yes, and I'd appreciate it if you'd keep a civil tongue in your head when you're referring to him."

Mickey's mind was catching up. "Wait a second. Did you say 'I don't have it'?"

"Yes, or rather I have it—we have it—but it's invested."

"Invested? Invested in what?"

"In art. Walter's expanded his gallery and his inventory."

"*All* of it's invested? Eight million?"

"Yes, or at least most of it, except for what we need to live on—oh, I don't know—you know I've never taken care of the money."

Mickey was trying to absorb it.

He didn't know how much time passed before Rachel said, "Are you still there?"

"Yes. Just speechless."

"I don't know what else to say, Mickey. I'd like to help you, but it is, after all, *my* money now." She paused. "I'll talk to Walter and see if we can work something out."

"Thanks. I'll talk to you soon." He hung up, stunned. He slumped against the back of his chair and sighed. If someone else had told him he wouldn't have believed it. *Walter Goldstein.* He'd appeared in New York two years before Mickey was indicted, saying he "hailed from Switzerland," and opened a gallery in Soho, Galerie de Bourée—named, Goldstein had told him more than once, for the producer of his favorite burgundy—with a staff of anorexic waifs and stick-figure young men who spoke with Continental-European-learned-proper-English-in-Great-Britain accents that were almost as affected as Goldstein's. He always drove a brand-new Jaguar and carried on about the 4,000-square-foot loft he lived in above his gallery. Built like an aging heavyweight fighter, he cut an imposing figure in his custom suits—always double-breasted—and matching ties and pocket squares with bold splashes of color that declared he was artistic.

Goldstein dealt in up-and-coming modern artists, offering the cachet of owning an original piece of artwork by an undiscovered genius who would one day be famous. He threw around comments like, "Reminiscent of a young Jackson Pollock," or "de Kooning-esque." Mickey pegged him for a charlatan who cruised the social set, preying on the wives of men who were real players, wives like Rachel who had nothing to do but spend their husbands' money on charities, clothes, decorating their apartments, and art.

Mickey thought back to the last time he'd seen Goldstein, a few weeks before the U.S. Attorney's Office busted him. It was at the UJA-Federation of New York's annual Wall Street dinner, a black-tie affair that anybody who was anybody in the Jewish community on Wall Street attended. Mickey had been a fixture at the dinners for over 20 years, the recipient early in his career of the Wall Street Young Leadership Award for the "rising star who exhibited uncompromising integrity in business and philanthropy," and only three years earlier the honoree for the prestigious Gustave L. Levy Award for outstanding leadership in the Wall Street community.

A few days before the dinner, rumors had begun circulating on the Street about a big insider trading case the Feds were working on. Just that afternoon, Charlie Holden, the Assistant U.S. Attorney in New York, had threatened Jack and Mickey on the speakerphone about a "Source X" inside Walker that was cooperating, finally bellowing that they were toast once Source X got done singing.

Mickey tried talking Rachel out of going to the dinner, right down to an hour before leaving for the Waldorf.

"Oh, will you stop it please. We've had this discussion 10 times. I spent $5,000 on this dress," Rachel said, sitting in their dressing room in a slip, having finished her makeup and putting on her earrings. "You know perfectly well that all the glitterati of New York finance will be there. All of your friends, all of my friends. It's the event of the year."

Mickey heard her words, but they sounded as if they were coming from off in the distance, because he was listening to his own breathing, wondering why it was so even, why he was able to stay so calm. He always managed to stay that way in deal negotiations, not through years of practice, but because he was born to it. But this was different. His entire way of life was potentially coming to an end, and his reaction, or lack of it, fascinated him.

An hour later he was entering the Grand Ballroom at the Waldorf Astoria. The entire main floor and the two tiers of balconies in the cavernous space, a re-creation of the Court Theatre in Versailles, sparkled with light from the glass chandeliers that danced off champagne-colored decorative plaster and gold leaf. The voices of the 1,600 luminaries, clad in tuxedos, evening dress and their most ostentatious jewelry, resonated off the four-story-high ceiling.

After the cocktail hour on the main floor, Mickey accompanied Rachel to the elevator to the first balcony. They entered the cluster of a half-dozen tables where they usually sat with her closest friends.

After the dinner, after the keynote speech from Mayor Bloomberg, after the speech from the honoree for the Wall Street

Young Leadership Award, after the speech from the honoree for the Gustave L. Levy Award, after the announcement that this year's dinner had raised $22 million for Jewish charities, Walter Goldstein surfaced.

Mickey was sitting between Steven Weisenfeld and Jesse Stern, their wives huddled next to Rachel at the adjacent table, when Mickey sensed a presence behind him and got a nose full of too much cologne. He turned and saw that Goldstein had commandeered a chair and positioned himself behind Mickey and Jesse.

"Gentlemen," Goldstein said, "a pleasure to see you." He clapped a hand on Mickey's shoulder.

"Walter," Mickey said, only half turning to acknowledge him.

Goldstein extended his hand to Mickey, who looked at it for a moment before shaking it. Steven nodded to him and turned back to look over the balcony at the ballroom floor. Jesse looked as if he wanted to jump over the railing as Goldstein reached out to shake his hand.

A moment later Goldstein said, too loudly, "Thank God they've stopped that ghastly practice of passing the microphone around so we can all stand up and pledge our contributions, eh, old man. Bloody barbaric, it was."

It struck Mickey as an odd comment. It had been 10, maybe 12 years since the UJA stopped that practice, well before Goldstein landed on the scene. It was as if he'd researched it as deep background for this role. Mickey nodded and smiled, knowing if he just humored the man and didn't engage, Goldstein would move off to another table for some more hand shaking and back slapping, then zero in on the wives.

But Goldstein stayed put, and Mickey felt Goldstein's hot breath near his ear, his voice lowered to a conspiratorial whisper. "Awfully sorry to hear the rumors about Walker & Company."

Mickey eased his head around. "You know the old saying."

"Which one?"

"Talk is cheap. And it's especially cheap when people gossip about money."

"Perhaps, but people are going on about insider trading."

"Is that what *people* are going on about, Walter?"

Goldstein's smile curled into a leer. "Yes. It's all rather lurid."

"A sleazy mind can sensationalize anything."

"They're saying the Feds are poking around."

"Routine. Securities firms always show their regulators internal compliance records."

Goldstein mouthed the word, "Routine." Then he frowned, affecting sadness. "I rather hope for your sake that another old saying isn't true, old man."

"And that would be?"

"Where there's smoke there's fire."

Mickey's back stiffened. He turned around and closed his eyes, determined not to respond if Goldstein continued.

"Well, gents, I'm off to circulate," Goldstein said a moment later, just as Jesse's wife stood up from her chair next to Rachel and walked off, presumably heading for the ladies' room. Goldstein went straight for it and sat down next to Rachel.

Mickey got a good look at Goldstein then. Double-breasted tux, a royal blue bowtie and matching pocket square, his dark hair slicked straight back and his chin raised as if he were FDR cradling his cigarette holder in his teeth.

Jesse leaned over to Mickey and said, "Look at him go. Always the same, with that coat-hanger smile and dripping with refinement."

Steven said, "The guy's a nobody. Anyone with a brain knows he's living larger than his means to create the image he's a player. Probably sleeps in his Jag because he can't afford any furniture."

Mickey smiled, eating it up, but said, "Oh, come on. He's harmless."

Steven said, "You come on, Mickey. The guy's a shark. I'm sick of him. This is about the sixth event I've seen him working this year. I happen to know from Rebecca that he's sold Rachel some of that mediocre crap he peddles at inflated prices."

How well I know.

Jesse said, "I've heard that his stuff is created by a group of journeymen painters who can mimic others' styles. Some's even done by accomplished forgers."

"That, and the fact that his artists are creations of Goldstein himself," Steven said. "He packages their avant-garde appearances and lifestyles for his customers."

Mickey said, "I hear his real business is dealing in stolen artwork."

Steven and Jesse both turned in their seats and looked at Mickey, waiting for him to go on.

"Heard from who?" Jesse asked.

"I'd rather not say, but a lot of top bankers, lawyers, and CEOs are collectors. Some tell me Goldstein is tapped into a worldwide shadow network of buyers who'll pay tens of millions for a stolen painting or piece of sculpture by a famous artist."

"They can't show it to anybody," Steven said. "Why would they buy the stuff?"

"The mystique of ownership," Mickey said. "Look around you, down on the floor. There's a mountain of ego sitting in this ballroom. Men who'll keep a one-of-a-kind masterpiece in a secret place inside their homes." He looked over at Goldstein again, watched him schmoozing Rachel, wondered how much this was going to cost him.

Now looking back on that night, it all made sense. Goldstein wasn't trying to sell Rachel art; he was selling himself. He must have known more than was in the public domain, maybe had a contact at the U.S. Attorney's Office. Or maybe he simply guessed right about the rumors that were circulating about Walker & Company and believed Mickey would get brought down. Whatever the reason, Goldstein had been making his move on Rachel that night. He'd done it shamelessly, too, out in the open, right under Mickey's nose, the SOB. And now the gold digger was living in *his* co-op, spending *his* money, and sleeping with *his* former wife. *Unbelievable.*

Mickey sat there in front of the phone for a few minutes, staring at the wall, still trying to absorb the situation. Then he started turning it over in his mind, because it stirred something in him. After another few minutes he said to himself, *It could work.* He stood up and walked over to one of the computers and logged onto the Internet to start doing some research.

Moravian White was in the bedroom of his apartment with the door closed, rocking his head to the reggae beat on his boombox, when he thought he heard a phone ring. He turned down Bob Marley. *Yeah, a phone.* He wasn't sure if it was in his living room or downstairs. His apartment was in a two-story redbrick building on Rockaway Parkway in Canarsie, Brooklyn, above the Yummy Yummy Chinese Restaurant. Yummy Yummy's takeout was supreme, their phone always going. He crossed the bedroom, opened the door into the living room and got blasted by the smell of garlic and Szechuan peppers.

It was his phone ringing.

"Hullo."

"It's me."

Jack Grass, phoning from prison, Jack always careful because sometimes his calls were monitored. Attica Prison, in upstate New York, Jack doing two consecutive 25-year sentences for murder. Same as Moravian's brother, Dontelle, in Leavenworth, Kansas, same as Lionel Preston in Lompoc, California. All guys he grew up with in the neighborhood.

Moravian's pulse picked up. "Yo, mon. Is time?"

"Almost. Halloween, give or take. I'll hear, then let you know."

"Uh-huh."

"I'm guessing that around that time his ex will know where to find him."

"I got da woman's address."

"Okay. Talk to you soon, old buddy."

Moravian hung up. He sat down, stayed quiet, let the call sink in deep and hard, like it should. Jack Grass, Lionel Preston and his brother, Dontelle, the three of them in jail because of getting ratted out by Jack's old Wall Street partner, Steinberg.

He'd never forget when his mom and dad moved the family from Jamaica to Canarsie when he was seven, Dontelle ten, how Jack, one of the big kids in town, took them under his wing. How Jack and his guys protected him and Dontelle from the Italian kids. Hung out with them on Avenue D and showed them how to play stickball, got them on his team, and not just because Jamaicans knew baseball, could hit and run, play the game like it was meant to be played, not like the faggot Italians who wouldn't slide on the pavement, worried about scraped elbows and raspberries on their asses, but because Jack was one of the good whites you could trust. A standup guy.

One of the whites who showed you stuff. Stuff like how to stand in the bushes to throw rocks at the Canada geese down in Canarsie Beach Park, so you wouldn't get seen by the old Italian ladies sitting on the benches who'd rat you out to the cops. Or took you over to the flats behind the factories off Dewitt Avenue where you could moon L trains going past, with open space to run if the MTA cops chased you, laughing your asses off when they did.

Then later, not just kids' stuff anymore, got you into deals. Deals with money in them. Deals like the valet parking operation Jack dreamed up over at Peter Luger Steak House. Got him and Splits Duncan, Lionel Preston and Booker T. Wilson jobs as car jockeys after Jack sold the maître d' on the idea of valet parking so their customers wouldn't have to drive all over Williamsburg looking for a space on the street or a lot that might close before they finished their dinners. Dontelle too proud to do it, missing out on 200 bucks a weekend in tips between him and the guys.

Then later into deals like Saturday night rides over to Manhattan to boost out-of-town Mercedes and Cadillacs for chop shops out by LaGuardia Airport. Dontelle smart enough to get some of that, each of them making a grand a night after Jack's 20% cut off the top.

Then after Jack hit it big on Wall Street, still bringing him and Dontelle into deals, like when he needed muscle to keep other bankers off his deals, or scaring people into shutting up, or even making them disappear if they wouldn't.

Next he remembered how Steinberg looked so cool and above it all in the witness box in that courtroom on Pearl Street. Sitting there in his blue suit, his sparkly cufflinks showing as he waved his little Jew arms around while he talked to that sweaty puke of a D.A., taking down Jack, Lionel and Dontelle.

Dontelle, his only brother. Not blowing Moravian off as a little kid, three years younger, as he did in Jamaica, but in Canarsie accepting his role as the big brother, Moravian's protector, maybe from seeing how Jack acted. Or maybe because their dad never stepped up to do it, and almost right after they got to Canarsie their dad took up with Silvia, the Haitian bartender from Zeke's on Avenue J, then disappeared.

Dontelle, who helped find Moravian a trade down at Foremost Carburetor on Remsen Avenue, steady work he'd hung onto through four recessions, half the people he knew getting laid off and him still working because of Dontelle. After Mom passing away, Dontelle sharing the apartment with him, even paying more than half the rent. And right after Moravian moved in, Dontelle going over to Shapiro's Paints on Flatlands Avenue and buying two gallons of a nice pastel blue color, Benjamin Moore, the finest paint you could buy, to fix up the apartment so they could live like men instead of animals looking at 20 years of cracks, holes and scratches on the walls from low-rents who lived there before them.

When he was sentenced, Dontelle holding his head high and accepting his medicine, not being a crybaby like Lionel Preston, who acted like the whole thing was somebody else's fault, sobbing, "Oh, God, oh, God, how could this happen to me?"

Dontelle now away for what would be the rest of his life, never gonna sit on a bench with Moravian in Canarsie Beach Park and toke on a joint of fine Jamaican Lamb's Bread weed and sip from a bottle of Chianti, paper bag over it, while they watched jets come in to JFK.

Never again. That's why he was talking to Jack, Jack thinking he was gonna do Steinberg for the money Jack had set aside with Bucky Pierson. But it was because of Dontelle. Because Moravian would never see his big brother again or get to enjoy his only flesh and blood left here in the States on account of it being robbed from him by Steinberg.

Moravian walked back into the bedroom and opened the drawer to his bedside cabinet. He removed his Glock and hefted it. He hadn't used it in a long time, but he would soon. *Dat bastard, Steinberg.*

CHAPTER 2

When the overhead lights in Lloyd Hall went out that night at 10, Mickey and Paul stood in front of their bunks in their room for the standing count, no moving, no talking, in accordance with the rules. After a few minutes, Sly stepped into the doorway with his clipboard and checked them off. Sly closed the door and they sat down on their bunks facing each other as if they were two college kids in their dorm room.

"I think my idea might work, but we'll need to refine it," Mickey said.

Paul nodded for him to go on.

"In 1911, an aristocratic Argentine con man named Eduardo de Valfierno, who called himself a marquis, hired an Italian carpenter named Vincenzo Peruggia working at the Louvre Museum in Paris to steal the *Mona Lisa*. Valfierno had previously hired a French art forger to make six copies of the *Mona Lisa*, then had them shipped to different cities around the world. After the well-publicized theft, Valfierno sold the copies for millions to collectors he'd previously lined up. Two years later Peruggia decided to sell the real *Mona Lisa*, and took it to an Italian art dealer who turned him in. By then it was too late for the millionaires who bought the copies, because Valfierno had disappeared."

Paul was grimacing. "I thought we were gonna do a real estate deal, or something like that movie *The Producers,* where we sell people 2000% ownership of a new play or a movie."

"Everything else we talked about requires major capital to get started. We don't have it."

"Yeah, but how're we gonna orchestrate somebody stealing a famous painting, then selling six copies of it in cities all around the world?"

"My idea for our deal is for us to do it with only one copy, and of a painting that's already been stolen and never recovered. We get an auction going and sell it to the highest bidder. I'll work my wealthy contacts who collect art and tell them this is my new life as a high-end broker of unusual merchandise. You'll play my client, a multimillionaire art collector who owns a stolen painting he's interested in selling."

"You've done this before?"

"No."

Paul thought for a moment. "So how much you think we can make?"

"Depends on the painting, but I'm thinking $20 million, give or take."

"You're kidding, man. Twenty million, for a single painting? No private individual, however rich he is, is gonna pay that much."

Mickey looked him in the eye. "How about Leon Black, CEO of Apollo Global. He's rumored to have paid $119.9 million at auction for one of four versions of Edvard Munch's *The Scream.* And Stephen A. Cohen of SAC Capital Advisors reportedly paid $155 million for Picasso's *Le Rêve.*"

Paul whistled. "So then you know guys who'd be interested, even for that kind of scratch?"

"I know at least a dozen men who are major art collectors, and as I thought more about this, I realized that at least a few of them might be tapped into the purchase of stolen paintings. And if they aren't, I know someone who could probably broker a buyer."

Paul shook his head. "It sounds really complicated. I just don't think we can pull it off."

Mickey stared him down, then said, intentionally giving his voice an edge, "We've been kicking ideas around for a month and we haven't come up with anything yet. This is the first idea that might have legs."

"Maybe, but where do we get the forgery, and what painting?"

"I know the man who can do it for us, and he'll have to be the one to choose the painting, depending on which one he feels the most comfortable he can reproduce."

"But how do we get to this guy? We can't exactly take a field trip to go visit him."

"We don't need to take a field trip. He's right here in Yankton, three years into an eight-year sentence for forgery and conspiracy to commit fraud. By now you know everybody at Yankton has a prison job, and our man's job is teaching art classes to the other inmates. René-Pierre Bouchard, housed over in Delancey Hall."

"Delancey? Isn't that the rehab unit?"

"Yes. He pays the guards to sneak him in booze whenever he falls off the wagon."

"Great. Just what we need, a forger whose hands shake."

"Relax. It can't hurt to go talk to the man, see if it goes anyplace. We can't get hit by a truck if we aren't playing in traffic."

Mickey and Paul spent the next two hours going through the printouts of famous art heists that Mickey had researched online, 27 in total, before mandatory lights out at midnight. Mickey was disappointed at first at how many of the cases were solved and the paintings recovered. But the next morning, as they crossed the grass toward Delancey Hall to visit Bouchard, Mickey was confident that Bouchard would be able to work with something on the list of three major heists of 11 paintings that Mickey carried in his pocket.

They were about 50 yards from Delancey when Paul said, "I don't know what I was thinking last night, being so negative. I mean, I'm supposed to be the optimist, right? The can-do guy who goes out and sells the idea. Relies on you to be the brains, the one who pokes all the holes in our plan, then figures out ways around them to make the deal work." Paul turned to Mickey and made eye contact, flashed a boyish grin. "I just want you to know I'm on board with this, man."

Mickey smiled. *He's selling me. Good.*

When they arrived at Bouchard's room, he was expecting them, sitting in front of an easel with a partially finished painting, the smell of linseed oil pervading the room. Close to a dozen other paintings stood on easels across the room, groups of almost identical copies of three other paintings. Bouchard smiled, his eyes turning up at the corners, a cherubic face. He wore a full beard trimmed to a point, and was bald on top, allowing his hair on the sides to grow well past his ears. When he stood to receive them, Mickey could see Bouchard was only about 5'5", completing the picture that gave him the nickname "Monet" at Yankton.

"Gentlemen," Bouchard said, extending his hand. "A pleasure to meet you both. Mickey, I have heard much of you, and Paul, I have seen you around the campus and heard good things of you as well." He winked at Paul as he shook his hand. He motioned to one of the two bunks. "Gentlemen, please, sit."

Looking at the row of paintings across the room, Paul said, "Wow, you're prolific."

"I'm grading my students' work. I have my advanced class copy the masters as a lesson in composition, color layering and brushstroke technique."

"Pretty good," Paul said.

Bouchard reached beside him and switched on a machine that projected an image of the painting that he was copying, crosshatched with hundreds of tiny grid lines, onto his work-in-progress.

"A rudimentary tool used in high schools and colleges throughout the country. It allows a student to project a painting onto her canvas and replicate it. None less than Leonardo da Vinci invented one such device in the 1500s. Sometimes it's hard to improve on what's been tried and true for hundreds of years." He smiled, his entire face participating in it. "Decades ago I devised the grid line system to allow me to copy a painting one square inch at a time. Nothing proprietary. It's in wide use today."

Bouchard switched off the machine and pulled his stool closer to them. "Now, gentlemen, I am excited about your project. Please tell me your ideas."

Mickey pulled out his papers and said, "The March 18, 1990, Boston Isabella Stewart Gardner Museum robbery—"

"The largest art theft in U.S. history," Bouchard cut in, "carried out by two bold men dressed in police uniforms and wearing imitation black mustaches. They banged on the door to the museum after 1 a.m. and demanded entry to investigate a disturbance that had been reported. Security guards let them in and were immediately tied up by the bandits. The men raced through the museum with skilled eyes, taking 13 works with them. Three Rembrandts, a Vermeer, a Govaert Flinck and a Manet. Five sketches by Degas, a bronze Chinese beaker and a bronze eagle from the top of a Napoleonic flag. The paintings alone were estimated at a value of around $200–$300 million. Even though the museum offered a $5 million reward, the paintings were never seen again. Yet, in 1997 . . ." Bouchard raised an arm and pointed his finger at the ceiling, as if for emphasis.

Mickey smiled and sat back, watching as Bouchard went on, gesturing and modulating his voice like an actor who's finally gotten a lead on Broadway again after being relegated to summer stock for a decade.

". . . The FBI raised two suspects, a convicted art thief named Myles Connor Jr., and his friend, an antique dealer named William P. Youngworth III. Both men were behind bars at the time of the theft, but were believed to have masterminded it while incarcerated. The men attempted to negotiate deals with the FBI for the return of the paintings in exchange for release from prison and the reward, but those efforts failed, probably because neither man was actually involved in the theft. None of the items has ever been recovered."

Mickey said, "Any possibilities?"

"The Degas sketches would not be my specialty to replicate. The other paintings, except for the three Rembrandts, are obscure, and I'm not very familiar with them. To attempt the Rembrandts would be sacrilege."

Paul said, "Sacrilege?"

Bouchard grinned and said, "My way of saying I couldn't do it. Too many fine brushstrokes, too many translucent, tinted layers of paint on top of each other. Too much time required for drying. The whole process would take months, possibly a year to produce an acceptable result with any of them." He held out his hands and opened his palms. Mickey observed his fingers: rock steady, no shaking. "And, even with my skills, I wouldn't presume to believe I could equal his artistry."

Mickey said, "Next on our list, Sweden's National Museum heist. On December 22, 2000—"

"A daring robbery," Bouchard cut in again. "The stuff of thriller movies. Three masked thieves, one armed with a machine gun, held up the museum near closing time. While the armed thief held the guards at gunpoint, the other two ran off and grabbed two Renoirs, *Young Parisian* and *Conversation with the Gardener*, and a self-portrait by Rembrandt. The three paintings were worth an estimated $30 million. At the same time the robbery was occurring, two cars exploded around Stockholm as a diversion, in addition to which accomplices scattered spikes on surrounding roads to further distract and delay police.

"More spectacular than what had already occurred, as part of their escape the three men jumped into a speedboat waiting for them at the waterfront museum and motored off into the darkness, disappearing toward one of the thousands of tiny islands around Stockholm. Within weeks, eight men were arrested; two of them were convicted of armed robbery, and another five of accessory to armed robbery. To this day, no one knows if these men were responsible for the crime. Years later, Renoir's *Conversation with the Gardener* was recovered during an unrelated drug raid. The other two paintings remain lost."

Mickey waited a moment to see if Bouchard was finished, then said, "Two possibilities?"

"The Renoir, yes. Then there's Rembrandt again."

Mickey said, "Next on our list, the Van Gogh Museum robbery in Amsterdam on December 7, 2002." Mickey looked up at Bouchard, ready for him to take over, but this time the man sat, smiling and nodding his head. Mickey continued. "Two thieves used a ladder to enter a window in the rear of the museum. They stole two van Gogh paintings, *Congregation Leaving the Reformed Church in Nuenen*, and *View of the Sea at Scheveningen*, valued at $15 million each. In 2003, police arrested two suspects, one a Dutch international art thief, Octave 'The Monkey' Durham, and an accomplice, who were found guilty of the robbery, in part because of DNA evidence."

Bouchard was nodding his head as if in agreement. He said, "Despite this fact, neither painting has ever been recovered."

Paul leaned forward on the bed, looking eager. Mickey said, "What do you think?"

Bouchard closed his eyes. "Ahh, van Gogh. I've done restoration work on many of his paintings, have studied *View of the Sea*, and even painted a copy many years ago for a collector. I can see the bold swaths of paint from van Gogh's rough brushstrokes on the canvas—an early work, before he developed his palette knife technique in his tormented later years. I could replicate *View of the Sea* without anyone knowing it isn't the original. I'd need a month or two to do it right. Mix the browns and grays myself, using oil paints I procured from the same French manufacturer that van Gogh used, tinted to mimic darkening with age. Add lead naphthalene to the paints to speed the drying, force them to crack a little as they did so, mimicking the minute cracks that have occurred over 120 years since *View of the Sea* was painted. Place grains of sand in a few strategic places that I observed the last few times I studied the painting: van Gogh painted *View of the Sea* outdoors on the beach—en plein air—at Scheveningen, a beach resort near The Hague." Bouchard opened his eyes and leaned forward to smile first at Mickey, then Paul. "It would be a labor of love."

Mickey nodded. "Sounds great. When can you start?"

"My fee is 20%. If you're agreeable, I can begin tomorrow."

Mickey looked over at Paul and nodded. Paul nodded back.

"Done, partner," Mickey said.

Mickey's first official act upon arriving in New York after his release was to walk up Park Avenue from Grand Central Terminal, wearing the midnight blue suit in which he was admitted to, then released from Yankton. The suit looked like he'd slept in it for two nights because he had, on a Greyhound bus from South Dakota to the Port Authority Bus Terminal. It was a crisp mid-October day, the suit just enough for the fall bite in the air.

He couldn't resist smiling as he crossed 47th Street, hearing the taxi horns, smelling diesel exhaust from the trucks, seeing men in gray-and-chalk-striped suits walking past him with serious intent in their eyes. He felt a glow as a young businessman in his late 20s walked past with purposeful strides, briefcase in hand, Mickey remembering how he'd been at the same age. Working at least 80 hours a week, feeling he was on his way, his only limitation the extent of his dreams. It made him think of his young insurance agent, Ryan Robbins. Ryan, only 25, earnest, with his firm handshake and solid eye contact, who always closed his emails with "Professionally," before typing his name. Mickey picked up his pace, energized.

He saw three middle-aged men in pinstriped suits approaching, engaged in serious conversation, either heading to a business meeting or discussing the results of one they'd just come from. He smiled again, enjoying it, feeling a part of the rhythm of New York business.

A moment later he sensed a sag in his chest, then realized it was a feeling of melancholy. This was a world he was no longer a part of. His former life. Not his new one, post conviction, post prison, post disgrace.

Now he felt like he was a fraud, masquerading as someone who belonged. He rolled his head downward to look at the sidewalk in front of him, afraid now that he might encounter someone he knew. He turned left on 51st Street to head toward the West Side and the nearest subway entrance from which he could head downtown.

When Mickey got downtown to Chelsea, he stopped into a JPMorgan Chase Bank branch and cashed a check for $1,000, almost a third of what he had in the account. Next he walked to a Duane Reade drugstore and bought a prepaid cell phone for $9.95, and a $200 airtime card. Then he walked over to B&H Photo and bought a used laptop Acer PC for $499.

On the way back toward Chelsea, he stopped at a men's store on 23rd Street and bought six each of white button-down dress shirts, underwear and black socks. He found blue, black and red pin-dot ties to complete his usual uniform with a dark blue or charcoal gray suit, and left the store feeling more optimistic. He figured the clothes would hold him until he could pick up his own wardrobe from Rachel. He checked into the GEM Hotel's cheapest room, $159 per night. When he got upstairs he logged onto the Internet and set up a free Gmail account.

Then he sat back and smiled, figuring he was in business. He picked up the prepaid cell phone and got ready to dial.

But who to call?

Paul in jail? *Hard to get anybody dialing in.* His lawyer? *Hardly.* He dialed Rachel.

"Hello?"

Hoarse. *Still smoking.* "It's Mickey. I'm out."

Rachel said, "I thought about our last conversation." Mickey paused, waiting. He didn't need a calculator to do the math. At $159 a night, his remaining $2,756 would hold out for 17 days. And that was if he didn't have to eat. "I have some money for you. It's not much, but at least it's something."

"Thanks, Rachel. Anything would help."

"And I think I figured out a place where you can stay for a month."

"Oh?"

"The Weisenfelds are in Europe. I agreed to check in on the place a few times a week, water the plants, take in the mail, so I have the key. I haven't asked them, but I know that Rebecca won't mind if you stay there, and, well, let's just not make a big deal about it or say anything to them for now."

"Okay." Mickey felt odd about it, but he realized he didn't have much choice, and was grateful for the opportunity.

"I can meet you in the lobby of their building at about 11 a.m. tomorrow."

"I'll be there. Oh, and Rachel, can you do me a big favor?"

"What's that?"

"Could you bring a couple of my suits? I've been wearing the same one for three days."

Rachel didn't respond immediately. After a moment she said, "I don't have them anymore."

"What?"

"I gave them away. After Walter and I were engaged he needed the closet space. I thought I could at least donate them to the thrift shop at the temple."

Mickey bristled at the image of Goldstein's suits lined up in his walk-in closet, then realized it made sense. She'd moved on with her life, so why on earth would she keep his suits in the closet of what was now her co-op? He thought for a moment. "How long ago?"

"About a year."

That was a long time ago, but because he'd owned a few dozen of them, some could still be there and it might be worth a try. Then he thought about the humiliation of someone from the congregation seeing him poking around in the racks and decided to forget it. He said good-bye and hung up.

Moravian White crossed 63rd Street on Park Avenue wearing a UPS uniform, a cardboard box under his arm. He arrived at the brass awning in front of the building, checked the number on the box, made sure it was right. *Number 575.* He'd bought the UPS label off of Splits Duncan where he worked at his UPS job down on Rockaway Parkway, had Splits set it up in the computer to make the package look official and all, in case anyone checked.

He hiked up his pants. They were too big, and the Glock in the pocket made them sag. He went inside the building, walked up to the concierge with a nice smile.

"Package for Mrs. Rachel Steinberg."

The concierge didn't answer, just held out his hand.

"She got to sign, personally."

The concierge gave Moravian an annoyed look. Moravian made his nice smile even nicer, shrugged like it was just the company rules, nothing he could do about it.

The concierge said, "Let me see." Moravian handed him the box. The concierge looked at it, handed it back and pointed to the elevator. "Ninth floor apartment B."

After Moravian stepped into the elevator and turned around he could see the concierge calling upstairs. When the doors closed, Moravian cinched his belt tighter, hiked up his pants again and stuck his right hand in the pocket to hold onto the Glock, the package under his left arm.

The woman seemed calm when she opened the door. She never looked Moravian in the eye, smiled or anything. Just held her hand out for the package and reached out to sign the little machine for the electronic signature that Moravian swung up from his belt, the one Splits charged him $200 to use for half the day. After she signed he handed her the box, then said in a timid voice, "Would it be okay if I got a glass of water?"

The woman looked surprised, then smiled and said, "Sure. Wait here." She turned and walked into the apartment. Moravian stepped inside and closed the door. He looked around, couldn't see anyone else. He heard her heels clacking as she crossed the kitchen floor, then the water running, then her walking back toward him. He met her in the doorway to the kitchen with the Glock raised in his hand.

Her eyes got big and her mouth dropped, then so did the glass of water and smashed on the floor.

"Don't say nothing, just listen."

The woman nodded.

"Anyone else here?"

She was too afraid to talk, just shook her head.

"Good. You don't do nothing funny, you stay alive."

She looked like she was ready to cry. This would be easy.

"Where is he?"

"Who?"

"You know who."

"Walter?"

"No, Mickey. Your ex."

She froze, couldn't speak again.

He moved closer, grabbed her by the collar and put the Glock against her cheek. "You don't tell me, you get knocked around, maybe even die."

"I—I don't know where he is."

He pulled her toward him, heard the sound of crunching glass under her shoes, then swung around and pushed her through the hallway toward the front door. He got her against the door, his hand still gripping her collar and decided to give her a little taste. He swung the gun back and smacked her under the eye with it.

"Oh my God!" she said and went limp.

Moravian held her up, said, "You want some more?" She had her eyes squeezed shut tight, but tears were now streaming down her face. He could see a lump already forming underneath her right eye.

"Open your eyes." She did it. They were full of fear. "You lying to me?"

"My God, no. I don't know where he is. Don't you think I'd tell you if I did?"

By how she was shaking and crying, Moravian figured she was telling the truth. He wasn't expecting this, couldn't decide what to do next, so he just shoved her away from the door. "I'm leaving now, but you call that concierge man downstairs and I shoot him dead, right in the lobby. You hear me? And then I come back for you. Or if you call the cops, I come back later and you're a dead woman. Understand?" He opened the door and left. He rode down the elevator with a lady carrying a baby. He acted like nothing happened, but he could feel sweat on his forehead.

Gotta think this through.

The next morning Mickey got to the Weisenfelds' apartment building, the Ritz Tower, on 57th and Park Avenue about 10:45 a.m., a shopping bag with his clothes in one hand, a soft computer case with his laptop in the other. He entered the lobby and walked up to the concierge, a big, friendly Latin man, Hector Rivera, he recognized from years of visiting the building.

"Hector, how are you?" Mickey said.

"Well I'll be," Hector said. He stood up. "A pleasure to see you—" he said, then stopping as if he'd forgotten Mickey's name.

Mickey shook hands with him.

"I heard about your troubles. Glad to see you're out and about again." Hector sat back down behind his desk and picked up the handset on the phone, ready to call upstairs. "Who're you here to see?"

"Nobody. I'm meeting Rachel, my ex-wife. We have some things to discuss, and she's arranged for me to stay for a little while at the Weisenfelds' apartment until I get on my feet."

"That's awfully nice of them."

Mickey nodded, then shifted his weight, feeling awkward about it. He saw Hector's gaze move past him to the front door at the same moment he heard someone entering the lobby.

Mickey turned to see Rachel emerge from the revolving door. He started walking toward her. She still had the same angular high cheekbones framing her sunglasses, no paunch or wrinkles in her face. Her hair was cut halfway to her shoulders as she always wore it, and her body still looked slim and toned. She wore a cashmere blazer and a skirt, with a scarf tied around the open neck of her shirt. *Still a great-looking woman.* It made him feel proud.

When she reached him she clasped one of his hands in both of hers and said, "Mickey."

Mickey saw that her face was tense, detected a slight tremor in her voice, and knew immediately that something was wrong. He felt a rise of alarm.

"Are you okay?"

"No. I've had quite a scare."

He took her by the hands and walked her over to the sofa in the lobby, sat her down. "Tell me."

"A man came to the apartment looking for you yesterday afternoon. He had a gun. He hit me in the face with it," she said, pulling her sunglasses off.

Mickey could see a welt beneath her right eye. She appeared to have covered it with makeup, but it was clear she had a pretty ugly bruise. "Do you know who he was?"

"No. He was African-American, very dark skinned, with a heavy Caribbean accent."

"What did the police say?"

"I haven't called them. The man said if I did he'd come back and kill me."

Mickey knew that was nonsense. How would the man know if she called the police? But he could see that Rachel was terrified. "What's Walter doing about it?"

"I haven't told him. He's in Europe for three weeks on one of his art buying trips."

It jolted Mickey into feeling even more protective of her.

"Let's get you upstairs. You should probably stay here, too. At least until we sort this thing out, maybe get you some police protection." He stood up.

She looked up at him, said, "I—I'm not sure."

"You can't go back to the apartment now."

"I'm not sure what Walter would say about the two of us staying in the Weisenfelds' apartment together."

Under the circumstances, the fact that Rachel would even say that meant the man was an even bigger horse's ass than Mickey thought. "Rachel, that's ridiculous. If Walter's and my situations were reversed, I'd want you to be in the safest place possible, with someone you know and trust. You're obviously still in danger. What would he expect you to do? Go to a hotel by yourself and sit around with the gunman preying on your mind? Go back to the apartment and wait for the gunman to come back? You'd be totally exposed there by yourself. Come on," he said, pulled her by the hand up from the sofa, and then ushered her toward the elevator.

———◇———

Upstairs, Mickey sat next to Rachel as she lay on the bed in one of the Weisenfelds' guest bedrooms. He insisted she tell him again exactly what had happened with the gunman in her apartment. By the third run-through he wasn't getting any new facts, so he left her alone. About five minutes later she drifted off to sleep. She looked elegant as ever, and yet so vulnerable. He reached out to stroke her hair, then felt a heaviness in his chest and pulled his hand away, realizing it was no longer his prerogative to do so. He tiptoed out and pulled the door shut behind him.

He crossed into the living room and looked around. He knew it well, a place he'd visited hundreds of times. Two three-foot antique Chinese jardinieres on either side of the doorway from the entry hall. A mixture of 19th-century antiques and Ralph Lauren furniture. Plush Oriental rugs. Custom-made drapes. Not too much different from the apartment he'd shared with Rachel.

He sat down on the sofa, now feeling like an intruder. He got up and walked into the kitchen, sat down at the granite island, feeling less out of place on the hard-backed stool. He pulled the cell phone out of his pocket and dialed information to get the phone number for the U.S. Attorney's Office in downtown New York. He called and asked for Charles Holden, the Assistant U.S. Attorney who had been Mickey's prosecutor—and persecutor—on his insider trading case.

"Charlie, it's Mickey Steinberg."

"Fully rehabilitated?"

Mickey ignored the sarcasm. "I need your help."

"You're barking up the wrong tree."

"Someone looking for me just roughed up my ex-wife. Pistol-whipped her with a gun."

"Not my department. Call the cops."

"This wasn't some random event. I told you, the man was looking for me."

Holden didn't respond.

Mickey said, "Somehow I don't think you'll look so good if something happens to Rachel—or me—and it was because you left a loose end dangling that's related to one of your own cases."

He heard Holden sigh.

Mickey said, "I guess you're right. I should call the police."

"No, don't do that. If you call the cops they'll think it's their investigation. I'll put a couple of my guys on it. We'll bring in the cops afterward, and that way we'll run the show. Where's Rachel living?"

"Our old apartment, 575 Park, at 63rd Street. But right now she's at a friend's apartment at 465 Park, at 57th Street."

"And you?"

"Temporarily at the same address."

"Nice setup for a convicted felon."

"I didn't call to impress you. What are you going to do?"

"I'll send a couple of my men up there. They'll get a description of the guy and put her place on stakeout. I assume she got a good look at the sleazebag."

Mickey told him the description Rachel had given him. Holden said, "Anything else?"

"She said he reeked of Chinese food."

Holden paused, then said under his breath, "Son of a bitch."

"What?"

"Dontelle White and his brother lived over a Chinese restaurant."

"Canarsie, right?"

"Yeah."

Mickey knew it had to be the case, and felt a chill.

——◆——

Mickey found a Post-it pad and wrote a note to Rachel saying that he went out to get something to eat. He took the key, stuck the Post-it note to the front doorknob, and left. In the lobby, he walked over to Hector at the concierge desk.

"Any idea where I can get something to eat around here on a budget? A diner or something?"

Hector said, "Yeah, there's a couple places, but you're in luck. I go on break in five minutes and my lunch's heating in the kitchenette. Homemade rice and beans. I got way too much for me and you're welcome to join me."

Mickey smiled. "That's the best offer I've had in a while." Five minutes later Mickey stood beside Hector over the stove in the kitchenette. Hector had two separate pots on the burners, one with yellow rice, the other with black beans. He stirred them and put the lids back on.

"I've always seen them mixed together," Mickey said.

Hector smiled. "You don't cook much, do you?"

Mickey shook his head.

"You never cook rice with anything in it. You don't mix the rice and beans until you sit down to eat, then you pour your beans on top of the rice."

A few minutes later Hector spooned out two steaming plates of rice, then the beans on top. One plate was piled about two inches higher than the other. He walked them over to the table, placed the smaller plate on his side and sat down.

"You gave me about two thirds of it," Mickey said.

Hector looked up and said, "I'm going home to a big dinner. Besides, you look like you haven't had a real meal in some time." He smiled, then looked back down at his plate and picked up a forkful. "Comfort food. Enjoy." A moment later, he said, "There are some exceptions to what I said before about never cooking rice with anything in it. My mother is Cuban, and she makes *Paella Cubana* that for her is like a religion. She puts the rice in a pot and simmers it with wine, broth, chicken, chorizo sausage, ham, mussels, spices and vegetables until the rice is cooked. Then she mixes in cooked lobster tails, shrimp and clams. To taste it could make even a Jewish man see Jesus."

Mickey laughed. "Sounds good enough to convert me."

They ate in silence for a while, and then Hector said, "Everything okay with Mrs. Steinberg? She looked like something was really wrong."

"Somebody roughed her up, looking for me."

"Mind if I ask why?"

"Something from my case. After we got indicted, my partner turned on me and sent some of his old friends after me to keep me quiet. So when I told the U.S. Attorney everything I knew, it put my partner behind bars for murder, along with two of his friends from the old neighborhood."

"So another friend from the old neighborhood paid Mrs. Steinberg a call?"

"Looks like it."

Hector glanced down at his plate and stopped chewing. He thought for a moment, then looked back to meet Mickey's gaze. "What're you gonna do?"

"Rachel will be staying here while her fiancé is in Europe. A couple of officers from the U.S. Attorney's Office should be here soon to investigate and protect her. The Assistant U.S. Attorney here in Manhattan thinks he might know who it was."

After another minute or so, Hector said, "Have you figured out what you'll be up to now that you're out?" That took Mickey aback. Not the kind of question he would've imagined Hector asking him in his former life. And yet, here Mickey was, sitting in the staff's kitchenette, the man sharing his lunch with him. *Lighten up*, he told himself. *This is your new reality.*

"No. As you can imagine, things have changed for me. I've got some thinking to do."

Hector said, "I don't know much about the circles you travel in, but a smart man like you must have lots of options and lots of people to help you out."

Mickey didn't respond right away, then said, "Not exactly. And it's the circles I *traveled* in. Past tense. Most of my former friends don't think too highly of me since I wound up in jail."

Hector nodded. "Yeah, I guess I can understand that. Well, you look like you're doing fine. Got on your standard getup, suit and tie, looking all put together."

"It's an illusion. It's my only suit, and it's not wrinkled because I hung it up in the bathroom with the shower running hot water for 20 minutes to steam it. An old trick I learned as a young investment banker on the road."

Hector nodded as if he understood.

Mickey picked up another forkful of rice and beans.

An hour later, Mickey rode the elevator back upstairs. When he entered the apartment, he saw Rachel sitting on the sofa with a cup of tea.

She smiled. "Thank you for listening. I guess I needed to vent. I'm better now."

Mickey didn't think so. The frantic look in her eyes was gone, but she now seemed dazed.

Rachel held up a two-inch-thick envelope. "For you. It's not that much, but it should help."

Mickey walked over and took the envelope from her. It was full of cash.

"Twenty thousand. From my personal bank account. It's the best I can do for now."

Mickey felt a twinge of guilt. "Thank you. I'll pay it back as soon as I can."

Shortly afterward, two men showed up from the U.S. Attorney's Office to interview Rachel. Both were wearing suits with bulges in their chests showing they were armed. Somehow it didn't make Mickey feel more secure. One man was tall and balding, in his late 50s, looking bored. The other was intense, scrutinizing Mickey, the apartment, and then zeroing in on Rachel. He took command, telling Rachel to sit on the sofa, then pointed to an adjoining chair for his partner. He sat next to Rachel on the sofa.

He looked over at Mickey and said, "How about you go out for a coffee or something."

Mickey scowled, walked into the kitchen and slid the pocket door closed. He put the kettle on the stove and started opening cupboards to look for tea bags.

About a half hour later Rachel slid the pocket door open and said, "Agent McCaskey wants to speak with you."

Mickey walked back into the living room, his tea in hand, and stood across the coffee table from the one in charge, who he figured was McCaskey.

"Have a seat," McCaskey said.

Mickey sipped his tea. "I'll stand."

"Suit yourself," McCaskey said. "You got anything to add?" The man was looking at Mickey as if he was guilty of something.

Mickey shook his head. "I only know what Rachel told me, all of which I'm certain she must have told you. But I'm sure this is one of Jack Grass' friends out for revenge. Holden told me he thought the description might even fit Dontelle White's brother, right down to the smell of Chinese food."

McCaskey looked at Mickey for a long moment, maybe expecting him to continue. When he didn't, McCaskey said, "Any of those denominators could indicate he was acting in consort with others."

Denominators? Consort? "You mean Jack Grass, or some of his friends, right?"

"An individual who uses tools of that nature generally isn't acting alone."

"Tools?"

McCaskey didn't answer, but wrinkled up his face as if Mickey was too ignorant to bother with. The other man said from behind McCaskey, "A gun."

McCaskey said, "And based on Mrs. Steinberg's description, one of a semi-automatic nature."

Mickey saw Rachel peeking out from the kitchen doorway, listening. He said to McCaskey, "Anything else you can tell us?"

McCaskey said, "We'll coordinate Mrs. Steinberg's statement with our other informations to develop a profile."

"Aren't you going to show Rachel mug shots or something?"

"We'll take our own advice about how we initiate our process." McCaskey stood up and added, "Irregardless of any other developments, we'll have two of our resources stationed downstairs, one in the lobby, the other outside the premises. Same at Mrs. Steinberg's apartment building. Holden gave me your phone number." He fished in his pocket and held out a business card. "Here's mine." He turned to his partner, nodded and they walked out.

Moravian was talking on the phone with Jack Grass, looking out the window of his second-floor apartment at Rockaway Parkway, when he saw a dark green Crown Victoria pull over to the curb and park in front of a fire hydrant. Two men in suits got out and walked directly toward his building.

"She don't know where he's at."

"You sure?"

"She so a-scared I don't think she lying."

Jack didn't answer.

"I still on it, mon. I find the creep," Moravian said.

"I'm counting on you," Jack said, sounding unhappy, and hung up. Moravian put the receiver back in the cradle and ran to his apartment front door. He listened for footsteps coming up the stairs, didn't hear any.

Must've gone into Yummy Yummy.

It could be nothing, couple of guys, maybe even detectives, stopping for some of Yummy Yummy's renowned Chinese. But maybe something. Maybe the cops were expecting something with Steinberg getting out of jail, maybe figuring Moravian would be hot for Steinberg, what with him having ratted out Dontelle and all. Maybe the Steinberg woman ID'd him from a mug shot.

The only way out of the apartment was down the stairs. Thinking that made his pulse pick up. He told himself to calm down. He started back into the bedroom to get the Glock, then decided against it. No sense getting grabbed by a cop with a gun on him.

Then he realized that if the cops collared him, they'd search the apartment and find the Glock anyhow. He darted back into the bedroom, pulled open the bedside drawer and took the Glock. He stuck it in the pocket of his pants, then ran back to the door. He listened again for footsteps on the stairs, now feeling sweat tickling his forehead.

He didn't hear anything, so he opened the door and got ready to walk down the stairs as casually as he could. Then he heard the door open from Yummy Yummy into the stairwell and his pulse really shot up. He pushed his apartment door closed as quietly as he could, now hearing footsteps on the stairs. He ran into the bedroom, opened the window and looked across to the fire escape on the building next door. The alley between the buildings was about five feet, so he'd have to crouch in his window and jump across about three feet to grab the fire escape. Not so far when you weren't worried about missing and falling 15 feet onto concrete.

No time to think about it.

He climbed onto the windowsill, let out his breath and jumped. He smashed his forehead on the railing as he grabbed onto the fire escape, heard the clang of the metal rattling and muscled over the railing and onto the floor. He could hear his breath coming in gasps as he jumped through the opening onto the ladder and rode it as his weight forced it down. He fell off as it crashed to a stop above the alley.

He got right up. *Okay so far.*

He walked through the alley toward the street. When he got there he forced himself not to glance to the left toward Yummy Yummy, turned right and headed south on Rockaway Parkway. Two blocks away he crossed the street, then stood, catching his breath, in an alley next to the Jew dry cleaners from where he could watch. He stood there wishing he'd brought his windbreaker, shivering and rubbing his hands together like a junkie, the wind whipping dust, leaves and litter up the alley at him.

Five minutes later he saw the two suits walk out of Yummy Yummy and get back in their car, no bags of Chinese food in their hands.

Damn. No takeout, and nobody eats that fast.

They had to be cops, most likely looking for him. He waited until the Crown Vic drove past, watched it disappear into the distance and then stepped out of the alley and headed back toward his apartment. He'd go back upstairs and grab whatever stuff he needed, then figure out where he could stay. When he got across from Yummy Yummy he turned his collar up to protect his neck against the wind, changed his mind, and kept going up Rockaway Parkway. He had the Glock. That was enough.

<hr />

Mickey had only been out for 10 days when they told Paul he was being released. Two days later, Paul picked up his street clothes, wallet, $534 in cash and his iPhone and left Yankton. When the Greyhound to New York City stopped in Chicago for a two-hour layover, Paul decided it was time to call Mickey. He had his feet up on an old wooden bench in the Greyhound Bus Terminal, hearing the swoosh of passengers' feet hurrying past, the din of voices reverberating off the 30-foot ceiling. The place was dusty and stale smelling. He loved it.

Out in the real world again.

He felt like a happy-go-lucky Labrador retriever bounding around the backyard, off leash. He was itching with anticipation as he dialed Mickey's cell phone, wanting to surprise him.

"Hey, man, I'm out."

"Great. How did you manage that so soon?"

"They gave me two months' credit on my six-month sentence for time served while I was awaiting trial, and the rest was time off for good behavior."

"Good for you. I'm getting set up. Not quite there yet. I had a distraction, but I'll be ready soon. How about you?"

"Raring to go."

"Working on your music?"

Paul felt a twist in his gut. "Yeah, sure." Mickey had given him a list of classical pieces by the big composers—Mozart, Beethoven, Mahler and other guys—to bone up on so he'd be ready for the role he'd be playing as a fancy-pants art collector.

Mickey said, "So you've been working on them enough that when I play some selections you'll be able to identify them?" Paul felt another wrench in his gut. *Can he tell?* Paul said, "Some. But then again, maybe I haven't worked at it as hard as I'd like."

Mickey chuckled. "Yes, I know how busy it gets around there at Yankton."

Paul was expecting him to ask about the artists and sculptors next—an even longer list, hundreds of pieces to memorize—then thought of the wines he was supposed to be studying, and decided to preempt him. He said, "Bouchard is almost done with the painting. Man, you should see it."

"How's it looking?"

"He's in the final stages, tweaking it with that projector he showed us. He does the final coats of paint grid-by-grid." He now recalled Bouchard's own words, "To make certain he not only captures the charismatic luminosity of the colors, but also mirrors the authentic boldness and flamboyance of van Gogh's brushstrokes."

He heard Mickey chuckle again. "Alright wild man, anything else before I see you in 24 hours?"

"More like two or three days. This bus is as slow as a Catholic girl from Poughkeepsie."

Paul hung up, resolving to get busy. He had a few days to catch up so he wouldn't disappoint Mickey when he got to New York. He pulled a wad of paper out of his back pocket, unfolded it and looked at the list of musical pieces. Then he tapped the iTunes app on his iPhone. He'd start with Mozart first.

That night it was Mickey's turn to buy Hector dinner. Hector was working the late shift until midnight, and Rachel always went out with friends. She still looked brittle, tentative from her scare with the gunman in the apartment. Mickey wanted to ask her to stay in tonight and watch a movie on TV, but he knew she'd insist on going out. He was also aware she didn't want her friends knowing he was in town, or worse, staying at the Weisenfelds' apartment with her.

Hector was already sitting at the table in the kitchenette when Mickey walked in with a bag in his hand from Nikolai's, the Greek deli on 59th and Lex. He pulled out two lumps of aluminum foil and started unwrapping them.

"What you got?"

"Gyros."

Hector raised his eyebrows.

"Beef, pork, chicken and spices with grilled vegetables, all wrapped in pita bread. A bellyful for only $7.95 each. Perfect for the hungry man on a budget."

As usual, they ate largely in silence, Mickey enjoying the food and Hector's companionship. Hector finished first. "I'll say it's a bellyful," he said, wiped his mouth with his napkin and then reached down into his jacket pocket to pull out a stack of photographs.

"My kids and grandkids. They all come over from the Bronx and New Jersey for our Halloween party." Mickey continued eating, watching as Hector laid them out. Hector pointed to the first row.

"My son, Rafael. Next, his wife, Nola, and three kids, Ralph, Jennie and Safina."

Mickey nodded and smiled.

"Next, my daughter Raquel. Then her husband, Raul, and two kids, Charo and Angel."

He moved on to the next row.

"My son Alejandro, his wife, Maria, and Manuel, Celia and the baby of the family, Rose."

Then the last row.

"Last, my youngest, my daughter Sabina and her husband, John."

Mickey swallowed the last bite of his gyro, wiped his mouth and said, "Beautiful family."

Hector said, "Any kids?"

Mickey shook his head.

"You don't know what you're missing. You should do it."

"I'm 55, too old to start now."

"I got a friend, married three times. His youngest kid is 10. He was 65 when he had him. Age doesn't mean anything."

"I don't know where I'd start."

"Find a young one."

Mickey smiled, then started wrapping up the remnants of his meal, took Hector's paper plate, napkin and aluminum foil as well, folded them up and walked over to put them in the garbage can.

He had his back to Hector when Hector said, "You still care for her, don't you?"

Mickey turned around. "You mean Rachel?"

Hector nodded.

"I guess it shows."

Hector nodded again.

Mickey walked over and sat back down across from him. "That time is past, though. She's moved on and she's engaged. Plus, I'm no longer part of that life."

Hector's face was sympathetic. Finally he said, "Go on."

"Not much else to say. Although I've decided I feel like an idiot staying here, at an old friend's who would probably be appalled if he knew." He shrugged. "And, yes, I know Rachel still has affection for me, because she's gone out on a limb to let me stay here."

"So does this mean you're moving out?"

"Yes."

"Where're you off to?"

"I don't know. But that's not really important."

Hector nodded. "I understand, Mick." He stood up and extended his hand.

Mick. Mickey stood, too. *I guess I'm one of the people now.* As he thought it he realized it was a good place to be. He shook Hector's hand.

"You're a good man, Mick. You're better'n the other folks who come around here. You've never looked down your nose at me or any other working man. You take care, now. Stop by when you're in the neighborhood, and let me know how it's going. And if you ever need anything, let me know. You need a place to stay, I'm good for it. Good luck."

"Thanks, Hector, I appreciate that."

CHAPTER 3

On the next leg of the bus ride after leaving Chicago, Paul listened to the classical playlist on his iPhone on "shuffle." He'd listen to the first strains of music, guess the piece, then look at the iPhone's screen to identify it, like using flashcards to learn multiplication tables in grammar school. After a few loops, he got pretty good at it, batting .450 or so. Then he realized that was a great average for baseball, man, but wouldn't cut it for the deal Mickey had planned. He focused harder. By the time the Greyhound reached the Pennsylvania border, he was batting .800 and could even identify Mozart's work from his characteristic chromatic progressions, and Beethoven's string quartets from their dark dissonance.

He liked the flashcards idea, so he adopted it for the wines that Mickey insisted he be familiar with. He knew a smattering about different wines, having started out like many with giant wines like zinfandels, eventually migrating to the finer flavors of burgundies, largely with help from a friend who was a burgundy fiend. But he had nowhere near the depth of knowledge that Mickey considered essential for his role in their deal. So he created flashcards, starting with the Bordeaux. He pulled out the copies of the *Wine Advocate* that Mickey had given him in Yankton. Then he wrote the wine's name on a rectangle of paper, then on the back the rank in the 1855 classification—first, second

69

or third growth—the region and type of grape, and some notes about the wine. Like *Château Lafite Rothschild,* and on the back, *first growth; Pauillac region; cabernet sauvignon, merlot, cabernet franc and petit verdot grapes; tannic when young, one of the world's greats when mature, with subtlety, silky long finish and exemplary of the power of cabernet sauvignon.* He studied them with the music pumping in through his earbuds, multitasking through Pennsylvania and New Jersey.

But as soon as the bus entered New York City, Paul couldn't stop thinking about Jennifer. He knew that any man in his early 30s had needs, but from comparing notes with his former colleagues on Wall Street, he'd realized his were more powerful than most. He decided he must've been some kind of freak of nature, because he'd never outgrown an 18-year-old's libido. Problem was, he couldn't keep his heart out of it. He fell in love, and that got him in trouble. There was no telling when a glance from a brunette across a bar or a glimpse of cleavage would change the direction of his life. And his bank account. Like Irina in San Diego. Or Kathy in LA. He'd been a sucker, lots of times, and knew it.

But Jennifer was different.

He'd met her about a year ago, on a fall day similar to this one. He'd forgotten to reset his alarm clock after daylight savings time ended, and that Monday morning when he stepped out of his apartment building's lobby, he realized he was an hour early from the time on the Citibank branch across the street.

A bonus.

It gave him time for coffee and the newspaper before heading downtown to the office, and he got on line at the Starbucks on the next block. He picked up a *New York Times* from the rack. He'd watched the night before as the Yankees lost 3 to 2 to the Tigers, down two games to none in the American League Championship Series.

He opened the *Times* to the sports section, unable to keep himself from reliving the pain. A-Rod had struck out three times. "A-Rod, pathetic," he said under his breath.

He thought he heard a chuckle from the person in line behind him. He pretended not to hear it and turned back to the paper. Cabrera had put Detroit ahead for good with a two-out double in the eighth that scored Avila and Infante. "Man. Cabrera, that damned Cabrera."

Now he heard a laugh from behind him and a woman say, "The man's a Triple Crown winner. What do you expect?"

Paul turned around to see a blonde, maybe 5'10", smiling at him through sleepy eyes. A size XL terrycloth sweatshirt drooped off her shoulders and she wore old-style terrycloth sweatpants with holes in them. Her hair was pinned up on top of her head, no makeup, like she was in disguise as a dumpy housewife. But full lips, flawless skin and dramatic green eyes gave away her beauty. The only element of her figure he could see through her baggy outfit was the shape of full breasts shouting the word *Tigers* at him from under her sweatshirt.

Paul said, "I take it you're not a native New Yorker."

"Troy, Michigan, and a Tigers fan all my life."

"Don't look so cocky, they're still five games left."

"That's the trouble with you Yankee fans. Twenty-seven World Series wins, historic franchise, blah blah blah. You just can't see what's in front of your faces."

"Like?"

"Moribund former stars. Young phenoms that aren't panning out. Mouth-breathing manager in over his head."

"Smart mouth. Let's see if your boys can back it up."

"Looks to me like they are. I think we'll sweep the Series."

Paul took a breath, ready to fire back, when a guy from the back of the line said, "Hey, we're dying in line back here. Do it on your own time, man. Move up."

Paul turned and stepped up to the counter, ordered his coffee. He waited for the Tigers fanatic to finish her order. When she turned from the counter he said, "So, a sweep, huh? That's a bet I'll take."

She extended her hand. "You're on." They shook.

"Paul Reece."

"Jennifer Ledgerwood."

"Join me for coffee?"

That evening, as they walked down the steps to box seats on the third-base line at Yankee Stadium, Jennifer said, "Wow."

Paul figured those words were on almost every man's lips as well, Jennifer wearing skintight blue jeans, flats and a tight cashmere sweater, showing off a body that could melt glaciers. Her blonde hair was pulled into a ponytail, extending through the open back of a Tigers baseball cap. When they entered the box, Paul first, apologizing as they squeezed through, the guys sitting there stood up and said, "No trouble," "No problem," with the enthusiasm of seventh graders.

"I'm impressed," Jennifer said after they sat down. "You weren't exaggerating."

"Like I said," Paul said, smiling. "Fifth row, right on third base, 40 feet away from your man, Cabrera. And this way you'll be able to get a good look at A-Rod, too."

Jennifer rolled her eyes. "Yes, and I'll have almost as good a view of home plate to see him striking out."

Paul liked the self-assurance in her voice, the way she made eye contact and held it, and how she leaned in to listen to him like she was genuinely interested in what he was saying. He also liked that she was aware of but not at all self-conscious about the way she turned heads, and how those green eyes drew him in and made it impossible for him to remove his gaze from them.

The tickets had cost Paul $250 each from Steve Lifshitz, who had dibs on his firm, Belcher Securities' corporate box seats on the first-base line for the game. Then he had to pay a guy from Ireland Clearing Corp., a securities firm one floor below Belcher in their office building, another $150 each to swap Belcher's first-base-line seats for Ireland's third-base-line seats. It was worth it just to be there with Jennifer, although he didn't learn much about her once the game started. She was a real fan, perching on the edge of her seat and focusing on the action, commenting on balls and strikes. Then standing and hollering at hits or defensive plays by the Tigers. But she didn't rub it in when the Tigers won again.

It wasn't until they had tea after the game at the same Starbucks where they'd met that he started to get to know her.

"So you didn't do anything with your master's degree?" Paul asked, sipping his tea.

"Modeling bathing suits got me through Northwestern undergrad. My parents never would have been able to afford it and my scholarship only paid about half the freight. So I rode the El from campus in Evanston down to the Loop in Chicago for modeling gigs three or four times a week."

Man, she's beautiful. "And you say you started modeling in high school?"

Jennifer nodded. She squinted, her eyes more serious, and said, "I finished with an undergraduate major in art history and a minor in English. The modeling was going fine, but I didn't really know what to do, so I stayed on for another two years for a master's in art history."

And smart. "And you couldn't get a job with that?"

"After I graduated I interviewed for some jobs in museums in downtown Chicago. I couldn't believe that all a master's degree got me was a starting salary of $50,000 a year and a position arranging museum displays, nothing to do with what I'd studied. I mean, I love the art, all of it, but setting up little placards in front of ancient Roman artifacts on tiered displays in glass cases? Instead I started modeling full-time."

And normal. "You moved to New York?"

She shook her head. "I stayed in Chicago for about five years, then came to New York after I got picked up by the Ford Agency."

"Sounds great," Paul said.

She looked away, pensive. "Yes and no. I'm still making good money, but I feel like I'm in a rut. The same thing for the last 10 years. I'm hearing footsteps, too."

"What?"

"Younger, firmer girls. Like Catfish Hunter once said, 'My 30s have taken three feet off my fastball.'"

Paul decided not to say anything, let her go on.

"And I miss my parents." She made eye contact with him again.

"Still in Michigan?"

"Yes. Dad's getting a little too old to swing a hammer anymore—he's got arthritis and a bad back from years of being a roofing contractor—and Mom's got diabetes. They're both slowing down. My sister, Kathy, lives in California, and she's got two kids. So it's up to me. I'm the oldest, anyhow."

"It's a heartache, huh?"

Jennifer nodded. "Yes. And I don't get back as often as I should."

Paul nodded.

They saw each other every other night for the next week. At the end of the week, Jennifer invited Paul up to her apartment for a drink after he'd taken her to dinner at Daniel. They talked until 3 a.m., snuggling together on the sofa. After kissing for a while Jennifer let out a long sigh. She stood up and walked into the bedroom. Paul followed.

The next day Paul couldn't stop smiling. Or stretching his back: and he thought *he'd* never outgrown an 18-year-old's libido.

They'd been a couple ever since.

So as he walked out of the Port Authority Bus Terminal, paid homage to the statue of Jackie Gleason dressed as Ralph Kramden outside, then turned down Eighth Avenue, he decided Mickey would have to wait. On 38th Street between Seventh and Eighth avenues, he stopped in front of a generic men's store, pulled out the *GQ* magazine he'd bought at the Yankton bus station and flipped it open. In the window he saw a shirt similar to the one by Dolce & Gabbana that Brad Pitt wore on page 58, with buttons only halfway down the chest and embroidery on the front. A pair of tan gabardine pants was on the manikin next to it, comparable enough to the ones Pitt wore on the magazine's cover. Paul walked inside. In addition to the shirt and pants, he found a $39 windbreaker with a turned-up collar reminiscent of the $500 model from Gucci that Johnny Depp was modeling in an ad on page 189. Paul's shoes, size-13 boats, were still in style and so he opted to keep them and just give them a shine.

He left the men's store with a bag in hand and took a room at the Comfort Inn on 39th Street to get a shower and a shave.

An hour later he stepped out of a cab at Bloomingdale's, feeling his oats. He walked to the men's department to find a tester of Eau de Lacoste Bleu cologne, one of Jennifer's favorites, and gave himself a few sprays, not enough to be overpowering. Next he went up to the women's department and bought her a string bikini—she was a bathing suit model after all—and went outside and hailed another cab. He figured he'd just show up and surprise her. By the time he reached her apartment building at 72nd and Third he was second-guessing his strategy about surprising her. He walked into her building feeling a flutter of nerves.

The concierge called upstairs, waited, then put the phone back on the cradle. "No answer." Paul sat down at the sofa in the lobby and called Jennifer's cell phone. It rang three times, then went to voicemail.

He called again, same thing. *What?* If she'd had it turned off it would've gone directly to voicemail. If she'd been on the phone, he would've heard that funny beep after the ring that indicated as such, then heard it ring out 10 times, then to voicemail. It was as if she'd seen his number, hit REJECT and sent it to voicemail.

He sat back down and waited. A half hour later he saw Jennifer hurry into the lobby wearing skintight jeans and a purple fitted suede blazer, heels clacking on the marble, her hair down on her shoulders and sunglasses sitting on top of her head.

By the time he got his head into the elevator corridor, she was already standing in the elevator looking out, her sunglasses now down on her face and the doors closing. He continued into the elevator corridor until the concierge said, "Hey, you gotta wait for me to call upstairs."

The concierge gave Jennifer time to get into her apartment, then called. No answer.

"Whattaya want me to tell ya? A woman walks in looking pissed off, it's a good bet she's pissed off."

Paul walked back over to the sofa and sat down, thinking. He called her apartment, got no answer, then her cell, and heard it go directly to voicemail. He got up and walked over to a Starbucks, had a coffee and read the *New York Times*. An hour later when he walked back to Jennifer's apartment building, the concierge waved him over. "She called downstairs a few minutes ago and said to send you up."

Paul rode up in the elevator feeling good about himself, his clothes not positioning him where he'd be if he had the money to do it right, but close enough. His hair was gelled back, he smelled great, and with daily access to the gym at Yankton, he was back in top shape. A man on a mission, ready for action.

When he got off the elevator and sauntered, a little slower than necessary, to Jennifer's apartment, she had the door ajar. She wore the same clothes as when she'd entered the lobby, and only minimal makeup.

"Hi, babe," he said, and smiled.

"Well, well, well. The man himself, survivor of the labor camps in Siberia." She didn't smile, just stood there.

"C'mon, babe, aren't you gonna invite me in?"

She stepped back into the apartment without a word, let the door swing open. She walked over and sat down in a living room chair, not looking at him, staring straight ahead at the wall. She crossed her legs and folded her arms.

Like the concierge downstairs said, pissed. He knew her well enough to know he wouldn't need to drag it out of her, that she'd get right to it. That was good. They'd get past it, and in a few moments she'd start to soften. And why not? He looked great, smelled great, and he was here.

He sat down on the sofa adjacent to her and she looked over at him, curious, like she was observing some new species of insect.

Paul started to feel a little twitchy.

She glanced at the Bloomie's bag in his hand.

An opening? Paul held it up. "Got you a present." He smiled, stood up and walked over to her.

"Thank you," she said as she took it from him and rested it on the floor.

He walked back to the sofa and sat down. "Aren't you gonna open it?"

She looked at him for a long moment, then fished her hand into the bag and pulled out the gift-wrapped box. She opened it and held up the string bikini. "A Calvin Klein." She observed the back of it. "They've got this proprietary stitch around the hook in the back that makes it almost impossible for it to come undone while you're swimming," she said, now observing *it* like it was an insect. "It's very pretty." She looked up at him again. "Thank you."

Formal, almost cold.

A thought hit him, and he glanced past her around the room for signs of another guy. Some new end tables and lamps, a new stereo set with piles of CDs beside it, but nothing conspicuous. *Maybe things are okay.* He relaxed a little.

Then Jennifer said, "Flowers would've done just fine. Flowers are never corny, never out of style. A woman likes flowers." She narrowed her eyes at him. "Especially from her boyfriend. A boyfriend who hasn't called in over three weeks, even in response to two messages from his girlfriend about a seminal event in her life she's aching to share with him, the man who says he loves her."

Paul felt his shoulders droop, realizing she was just getting started. *Here we go.*

"A boyfriend who doesn't even call his girlfriend to let her know when he's getting back into town, allow her to get ready, maybe even plan something special for him."

"Something special?" Paul said, trying to latch onto anything to divert her. He leaned forward and smiled, trying to show how eager he was. "Great, like what?"

"Is that all you can say? Have you been listening to me at all?"

"Look, I'm sorry. I screwed up. I wanted to surprise you. And I'm kind of broke, so all I could afford was a dumb bathing suit—"

"I don't care about the bathing suit. I already told you, flowers would've—"

"—but I know you like bathing suits, even though you've got dozens of them—"

"Hundreds."

"—okay, hundreds."

With that Jennifer uncrossed her legs, unfolded her arms and placed her hands on the arms of the chair. She leaned forward and yelled, "For a smart guy you're incredibly obtuse sometimes, you know that? When you didn't call and just showed up unannounced, I was mad. But after stomping around the apartment for half an hour I started to cool off. Then I listened to your voicemail on my cell phone, 'Hey, babe, I'm back, blah blah blah,' as if nothing's happened and it sent me off the reservation again." She was standing and yelling at him now, her lips taut and the muscles in her neck showing. "As if I'm not supposed to feel totally taken for granted, treated as if I'm some vacuous bimbo who you expect to fall all over herself because you're back!"

Paul had heard enough. He felt a burst of anger, stood up and shouted back, "Alright! I said I'm sorry. What else do you want me to do?"

Jennifer froze, then sat back down. She took a moment to collect herself. While she did, Paul sat back down, too. Jennifer sighed and softened her eyes. She said, "I want you to listen to me. Let me tell you my news. To talk to me. Tell me your news."

Paul got up and stepped over to her, knelt beside her chair and took one of her hands in his. He could smell her perfume, the shampoo on her hair. "I love you," he said, meaning it. "Okay, you first. Tell me your news."

"I love you, too, but you're a dufus sometimes, you know that?"

"Yeah, I know." He smiled. "Go on, I'm listening."

He saw her exhale, her eyes soften more. She said, "You know that Victoria's Secret Angels commercial I told you about?"

"Yeah."

"I got the job. Only as an extra in the back, wearing those ludicrous wings, but they saw enough of me to like me, and they gave me a gig for some print ads."

"That's great, babe." He squeezed her hand.

She smiled for the first time. "There's more."

"And?"

She smiled again, broader now, like she was proud of herself. "And I'm not doing bathing suits anymore. I landed a regular gig as a Victoria's Secret Angel. I'm flying out tomorrow morning to Saint Martin for a three-day shoot for the spring lingerie catalog."

Paul leaned forward and kissed her. He said, "That's fabulous. Just fabulous. I'm so happy for you."

She reached up and cupped his face in her hands. "It's my big chance, and maybe my last shot to make it big."

"Last shot? Where's that coming from? It's just the first step. You're on your way."

"Come on, honey. I'll be 29 next month. They can airbrush out crow's feet, but my boobs start to drop and I'm done."

Paul laughed. "We should celebrate."

She pulled him toward her and kissed him. He started to lift her out of the chair and she dragged him onto the floor, rolled on top of him.

"We're staying in tonight. But I can't stay up too late. I've got an early flight to catch in the morning, and I mean it, Tarzan." She kissed him again.

Mickey had rented a room for Paul and him at the Chelsea Hotel on 23rd Street. It was twice as expensive as some of the other monthly apartment hotels he'd investigated, all dives, so the extra money for the Chelsea would at least let them feel human. The hotel was a 19th-century New York City icon, where artists, musicians, photographers, producers and composers were long-term tenants. Artwork, much of it painted by resident artists, some of it accepted in lieu of rent, lined the walls of the narrow hallways and adorned the rooms.

The space Mickey rented consisted of one central room with a foldout sofa bed, a separate bedroom and an ample-sized bathroom. It would do just fine. He'd bought a hot plate and set up a kitchenette area off to one side, even bringing in a mini refrigerator that he had to tip a kid from Bed Bath & Beyond $20 to carry up three flights of stairs. He'd set out a stack of used art books he bought from the Strand Bookstore on Broadway, a boombox-style CD player with a stack of mixed classical CDs next to it, and six bottles of wine with paper bags taped around them to obscure their labels. The smell of fresh coffee from the drip pot he'd bought permeated the room.

He felt elated, tidying up after Paul had called that morning to let Mickey know he was in the city and on the way. When he heard the knock on the door he strode toward it with a tingle of anticipation in his chest that he hadn't felt in some time, because this represented the commencement of their deal. As he put his hand on the doorknob he turned back to survey the room. *Ready.* Then he asked himself, *But is Paul ready?*

He opened the door to see Paul standing with a big smile, smelling of soap and cologne and wearing a European-cut suit with a shirt and tie. He held a garment bag over one shoulder, a knapsack on the other and a large book under one arm.

"The Chelsea," Paul said. "Sweet, partner. I didn't know you were so avant-garde."

"Yes," Mickey said, "Dylan Thomas wrote poetry while living here near the end of his life, Arthur C. Clarke wrote *2001: A Space Odyssey* while living here, and Mark Rothko and Willem de Kooning lived and painted here. I thought the venue was appropriate for the artistic nature of the deal we're planning."

"Yeah, and Dylan, the real Dylan stayed here, too. And Leonard Cohen boffed Janis Joplin here and wrote a song about it. And Sid Vicious stabbed his girlfriend to death here."

Mickey was taken aback a moment, then said, "Let me help you with that," and reached out to grab the book from under Paul's arm. "Welcome home."

They had coffee in the sitting area and caught up. Mickey decided he had to tell Paul about the man who had assaulted

Rachel while looking for him. Paul took it straight-faced, Mickey remembering Paul had been a cop. Paul told Mickey about his reunion with Jennifer, her recent triumph with Victoria's Secret and showed Mickey the book he'd borrowed from her apartment, Janson's *History of Art*.

After a half hour, Mickey said, "Okay, so how about we get started?"

Paul put his coffee down, nodded and stood up. He started to take off his jacket.

"No, don't," Mickey said. "Let's do this with you in character as our art collector, Paul Hilton."

"Hilton?"

"Yes, we can't use your real name. One Google search by one of our buyers and your Belcher Securities days and your sentence to Yankton will pop right up. Even a second grader would figure out that you and I cooked up some scheme while we were there together."

"Shouldn't we change my first name, too?"

"Too easy for someone to slip and call you Paul. You're Paul Hilton."

"Great, let's get started. Alright, man, hit me with your best shot."

Mickey said, "Okay let's try some wines first."

Paul nodded and swaggered over to the coffee table looking confident. Mickey hoped he was just hamming it up, in character as the hotshot art collector.

Paul picked up the first bottle.

"What is it?" Mickey asked.

Paul looked over at him, confused. "The label's covered."

"Yes, but look at the shape of the bottle. What kind of wine?"

"Bordeaux or a Bordeaux-style California wine, probably a cabernet, but it could be a zinfandel or a merlot."

"Could it be a burgundy?"

Paul shook his head. He pointed to three other bottles with sloping necks. "No, but one of those is. Either that or a California pinot noir. I know that gradual curve up into the neck instead of the more rectangular one on this Bordeaux bottle into a straight neck. I'm not a complete novice."

"Good. Okay now, pour the first wine, check the bouquet and taste it."

Paul poured wine from the first bottle, then made a bit too much of a display of swirling it in the glass, then getting his nose into it and sniffing. "I'm getting cherries, vanilla and tar." He took a sip, swallowed.

"The first sip is to clear your palate," Mickey said. "The second is to really taste it. Now take a big mouthful, hold it in your mouth for three full seconds, let it flow all over your tongue to hit all your taste regions."

Paul took a long sip, waited as Mickey went on.

"Your taste buds for sweet flavors are on the tip of your tongue, bitter in the back and sour and astringent on the sides. You need to hit all of them to get the true character of the wine."

Paul swallowed, then closed his eyes. He said, "Powerful. A huge wine. Massive extraction. Unctuous."

Mickey frowned and shook his head. "You were doing okay until 'Massive extraction' and 'Unctuous.' You're overdoing it, like a kid tasting his first glass of zinfandel. Take it down a notch, or they'll peg you as a phony or a pretentious fool."

Paul grinned. "Pretentious is good." He took another long sniff and another mouthful, waited, then swallowed. "It's a big California cabernet."

"Very good," Mickey said. "A 2007 Silver Oak."

Paul did a credible job with the rest of the wines. He could tell the French burgundy from the California pinot noir. He totally missed on the Châteauneuf-du-Pape, thinking it was a California syrah or petite syrah, but he identified the last wine, a Château Gruaud Larose 1989. "Wow, that's a great one. A well-aged French Bordeaux. Big, but silky smooth. Long finish." He buried his nose in the glass and took another sniff. "I'm getting cherries, vanilla and tar."

Mickey laughed. "That's the same thing you said about the Silver Oak."

Paul said, "Exactly. After reading all those issues of the *Wine Advocate* you gave me, I figured out that these wine writers' descriptions of every wine sound the same after a while. They use the identical words to describe the flavors, aromas and all that, but they just mix up the order. I can do the same thing—just fill in the blanks at random—and nobody will suspect that most of the time I have no idea what I'm talking about."

Mickey laughed again.

"Hey, man, how about, 'Oodles of jammy fruit, with prominent flavors of blackberry, tar and cherry, and subtle undertones of vanilla and licorice, followed by a long finish characterized by hints of jasmine flowers and apricots'?"

Mickey smiled.

Paul went on. "And maybe throw in some comments like 'Dominant tannins that will mellow with a decade of age,' or 'Solid acidity adding to the complexity,' here and there. You just need to put it out there with authority."

Mickey blinked his eyes, thinking. "Did you study up on the white wines?"

Paul shook his head. "Oh, the whites, they're merely pleasing aperitifs. The real glory of wine is in the reds."

"I'd say you're about ready for a trial run."

Paul was just as hot with the musical selections. Mickey loaded CDs into the boombox and started playing individual pieces of music, then asking Paul to identify them. He had a great command of Mozart, knowledgeable about most of the pieces in *Eine kleine Nachtmusik*, able to identify his key piano concertos, nos. 9, 15, 22, 27, and the famous *Elvira Madigan*, no. 21 in C major. He could identify each of Mozart's major symphonies, even some of the obscure ones he'd written when he was a young man, nos. 1, 4, 6, 8, and 9. At one point Paul stopped Mickey and said, "Most people gravitate toward Mozart's symphonies no. 40 and the famous Jupiter—Symphony no. 41—but I find the unusual dissonance and somber character of Symphony no. 39 makes it special. Somehow it even reminds me of his *Requiem*."

He was solid on Beethoven's symphonies and other work, too, picking out about a dozen piano concertos and sonatas—*Für Elise* was his favorite—and able to instantly identify Beethoven's string quartets. "Sometimes they give me the creeps, though," he said.

He could identify Bach's *Brandenburg Concertos*, a mix of Mahler's big symphonies, some Brahms symphonies and piano pieces, Tchaikovsky's famous ballet pieces and most of Chopin's preludes and polonaises.

After an hour of drilling him, Mickey said to Paul, "Pick one piece for me to play and tell me why it's a favorite."

Paul instantly fired back, "The second movement of Mozart's *Clarinet Concerto in A major*. They used it in the score for the movie *Out of Africa*. It can bring you to tears."

Mickey was pleased. He had a lot to work with here, and Paul was way ahead of where he thought he would be at this point.

Then they went on to the artwork.

So much for being ready for a trial run. Paul couldn't tell Manet from Monet. When Mickey opened Janson's *History of Art* and started showing Paul prints, he couldn't say whether Miró's *The Tilled Field* was surrealism, abstract expressionism, or impressionism. After an hour of futility, Mickey was convinced that if he'd used a multiple-choice format, Paul would've guessed existentialism.

"We get up early tomorrow," Mickey said, closing Janson, "and head up to the Metropolitan Museum of Art. You'll need to know a smattering of everything." He rapped his knuckles on Janson. "But it makes sense for you to have a predominant interest in one period. A man who's into van Gogh is obviously a fan of impressionism."

The next morning Mickey and Paul entered the Met shortly after it opened and rented players and headphones. They took the guided tour through the Lehman Collection, packed with impressionism. When they got home that evening, Mickey opened Janson again and marked about two dozen pages with Post-it notes. "Okay, wild man, you study. I'll open a can of something and heat it up for dinner."

The next day was the same. On the third morning as they left the Chelsea for the Met, Paul turned to Mickey with his boyish smile and said, "I'm psyched. This is starting to be really fun."

Mickey smiled as he turned away. *Ever the salesman.* The man probably felt like he'd be getting dragged through sticker bushes for the third day in a row, and he was crowing like he'd be going to a World Series game. He couldn't fault Paul's enthusiasm, but he hoped when the crucial time came, whenever it occurred, that Paul's natural bravado wouldn't cause him to put his foot so far into his mouth that it blew the deal.

Faking it with wines was one thing. Mistaking Brahms for Berlioz was another. But calling a Seurat a Renoir with a man you were trying to sell a $20-million stolen van Gogh could be fatal.

"This should be fun," Rachel said to Mickey.

"Yes," Mickey said, pleased she'd accepted his invitation. With Goldstein still in Europe on his buying trip, it made him wonder: did he have a chance with her again? "Hector tells me it will be quite an adventure."

"It already is for me." Rachel turned to look at Mickey "I haven't ridden the subway since you and I were new."

"I've already gotten used to it again."

They were seated next to each other, rocking with the motion of a No. 2 train on the way out to the Park Slope section of Brooklyn to attend Hector's family Halloween party, an annual event. Hector had told Mickey he was welcome to invite Rachel, explaining that he'd gotten to know Rachel much better now that she was staying at the Weisenfelds' apartment. Rachel was dressed in an outfit she might have worn out to dinner and the theater, a blazer over a shirt with a Hermès scarf around her neck, a long skirt and heels, evening makeup, so it even felt like a date. Mickey wore his suit and tie.

Mickey said, "Hector said that each neighbor tries to outdo the others. Displays, lights, sound effects, animated ghosts and goblins. Every year a new theme. And in the weeks prior to Halloween, they get tens of thousands of visitors who come from all over to see the spectacle. It started about 20 years ago, when young bankers, lawyers and other professionals started moving from Manhattan to Park Slope and fixing up old brownstones."

"I remember. People who moved out there were real pioneers. Park Slope was like the wild west in those days."

"Yes," Mickey said. "The first yuppies."

Rachel smiled and chuckled. "That was us in those days, too."

"Yes, but we were never adventuresome enough to try anything like Park Slope."

"You were always the more conservative of the two of us. But as I recall, every once in a while I got you to get a little wild." She smiled at him and held his gaze for a long moment. Mickey felt the warmth in it. Then she looked away and they rode in silence.

They got off the subway at Grand Army Plaza and Mickey directed them toward Hector's street, St. Johns Place. It was now dark, and parents were escorting their children on their trick-or-treating. The sidewalks on Union Street were crowded with Spidermen, ghosts, policemen, ballerinas and hobos.

Mickey noticed that Rachel now seemed pensive.

"You know, I never asked you why you did it," she said.

"You mean got myself into the mess I did?"

Rachel nodded.

"I've asked myself the same thing, and had plenty of time to reflect on it. It's hard to describe, but there's a certain thrill you feel when you step up to that line you know you should never cross, and then lean over it and taste a little of what's on the other side. Once you're over there, you realize it's downright intoxicating. And then it's no longer possible to step back."

Rachel was silent, letting him take his time, seeming to want to hear everything he had to say about it.

Mickey went on. "I was honest my entire life, totally strait-laced."

"To a fault. I learned very early on not to ask you what you thought of a new haircut."

Mickey looked over at her and smiled. Rachel smirked back at him.

Mickey continued. "So after I crossed that line, I understood that the straitlaced life was a thing of the past. So since I'd screwed it all up already I might as well make the most of the dark side."

They walked in silence for a while. Then Rachel said, "I'm glad my father didn't live to see you arrested."

Mickey wanted to say that Feldman would have been beside himself with glee, telling Rachel "I told you so," but he remembered the many times he'd seen the hurt expression on her face when he'd cut down her father. "Me too," was all he said.

"So what now? Have you and this young fellow, Paul, come up with any ideas to team up together on?"

"We're kicking a few things around. He's in the same basic situation I am. Ex–Wall Street, with no way to go back there again. Our options are somewhat limited."

"I hope you're not going to get in trouble again."

"So do I."

Rachel turned her head and looked him in the eye. "I meant I hope you're not going to do anything stupid that might get you into trouble again."

They continued walking in silence. The sidewalks were more crowded now that they'd turned onto Eighth Avenue. About a block later, Mickey said, "I was a little surprised—pleasantly so—when you agreed to come."

"Why?"

"I recall you saying how awkward you were at first about the two of us staying at the Weisenfelds' apartment together. You weren't sure how Walter would feel about it."

"I'm a grown woman. There's a big difference between sleeping under the same roof and going out to a party together." She hooked her arm through his. "Besides, you've always been my best friend, and there's no reason you can't still be."

Paul and Jennifer rode toward Park Slope in a Lincoln Town Car from Jennifer's car service. She'd returned from her shoot in Saint Martin late the night before, and she and Paul hadn't seen each other since she'd left. Paul could feel the sexual energy in the car, remembering the scene from *No Way Out* where Kevin Costner and Sean Young go at each other in the back of a stretch limo. He wished they were in a stretch now, with a privacy panel they could raise so the driver couldn't see into the back. He knew Jennifer felt the same way from how she sat close, held his hand and caressed his arm.

Paul had been telling her more about Mickey. "He's as smart as his reputation, but a regular guy, too."

"If they put him away for insider trading he can't be that smart."

"Even smart guys get caught."

Jennifer shot him a look, her eyes wide, and let go of his hand. "I meant he can't be that smart if he did it in the first place, not because he got caught. What's wrong with you?"

"You'll change your mind when you meet him. He's a really interesting guy."

"I'm sure he is. I'm just concerned that if you two are going to be partners on some deal, that you don't let him talk you into something illegal. Remember the spot your former pals at Belcher got you into."

"That was different. Those guys were crooks—"

"You didn't see it and they dragged you down with them."

"—but Mickey was duped by his partner at his old firm." Paul smiled at her to hide the fact that he was starting to feel painted into a corner. "Wait until you meet him, you'll see what a great guy he is. We're gonna do something special together, I can feel it."

Jennifer looked at him like he was her dumb little brother. "I've read up on him. You're hanging around with a man who confessed to being the architect of turning his investment bank into a giant insider trading machine. Watch your step."

Paul realized that at some point he'd need to tell Jennifer he was more than some rube from out west who the guys at Belcher corrupted. And with what Mickey and he were planning, eventually he'd have to come up with a cover story for her that would hold water indefinitely. That, or kiss her good-bye.

Now Paul wondered why he hadn't asked Mickey what he would say tonight about what the two of them were working on, so he wouldn't say anything that would be conflicting.

Almost as he thought that, Jennifer said, "So what's the deal with you two?"

Oh, man, Paul thought. He realized there was no hiding from her. *Sometimes things sneak up on you; sometimes they just slap you in the face.* Looking into Jennifer's eyes, he knew she hadn't asked it as a casual question. He wondered if she'd guessed what he'd been thinking moments ago, now understanding he couldn't face the prospect of kissing her good-bye. No deal was that important. He took her hand. Then he started talking.

As Rachel and Mickey walked up Eighth Avenue, Mickey could see the throngs of people spilling out onto the avenue from St. Johns Place.

"Get a load of this," he said to Rachel. The crowds grew thicker. As they walked closer, he could see two NYPD squad cars parked on Eighth Avenue, their lights flashing. The police had positioned emergency flares in front of barricades to block vehicular access to St. Johns Place. As they approached, Rachel and Mickey had to slow almost to a standstill to work their way through the crowd. When they turned the corner onto St. Johns Place, Rachel said, "Oh my God, Mickey, can you believe this?"

She sounded like she had as a twenty-something, looking out the window of Café Donato and laughing in amazement at a man riding a bicycle down Broadway in only Jockey briefs in mid-December. That was when he'd just started dating her. She was working at Macmillan in the Flatiron Building. Mickey would be at work and decide he needed to see her, tell Francesca to cancel any meetings or conference calls for the next hour, and jump into a cab down to Broadway and 21st, then insist that she take a break at Café Donato on the street level of the Flatiron Building.

Those were the days.

Mickey took in St. Johns Place.

It was classic old Brooklyn. Trees lining the street, wide bluestone sidewalks in front of brownstones restored to perfection and set back at least 20 feet behind wrought iron railings, with stone staircases framed by more wrought iron railings to elevated front doors. The brownstones were bedecked with an explosion of lights and decorations, each with its own Halloween theme. One was Charlie Brown, with floodlights planted in the grass between the street and sidewalk, shining up on the three-story brownstone. Schroeder and Linus looked down from the third-floor wrought iron window gratings, Pig-Pen and Snoopy, with Woodstock on his shoulder, were on the second floor, and Charlie Brown and Lucy commanded the first floor. The music from one of the Charlie Brown television specials spewed from speakers mounted someplace.

Another brownstone across the street was a ghoul's paradise. Manikins of goblins and zombies sat on the railings in front of the house and the steps, dismembered hands and heads protruded from windows, an animated body careened back and forth between the second-floor windows, and a loudspeaker declared that "All who approach will be fed to the rhombus in the backyard."

Mickey said he remembered a rhombus from high school math as some kind of quadrilateral with four equal sides.

Rachel said, "Then I'm staying away from that house. Math ate me alive all my life."

The streets were almost impassable, full of costumed children and adults. Mickey didn't know what was filling his senses more: the brightly colored Halloween lights, the soundtracks of the displays booming from speakers, the buzz of the throngs of people packing the streets and sidewalks, the smells of cinnamon, apple cider and artificial smoke, or Rachel laughing and smiling spontaneously.

He looked over at Rachel, who now held his hand in hers. "Hector didn't overpromise," she said.

A teenager dressed as Dracula approached them, fake blood on his fangs, and growled at Rachel. She clutched Mickey's arm in both her hands, laughed and called out, "Oh, don't take me yet, master!"

Mickey smiled and continued to push through the crowd, checking the numbers on the brownstones until he saw number 236, decorated from top to bottom in a vampire theme. He walked up steps hollowed with wear to a classic 19th-century brownstone, and approached a petite woman in her 80s. She stood in the doorway clutching a bowl of candy in one arm, handing it out to costumed children that surrounded her. Mickey saw Hector standing 10 feet into an entry hall ablaze with lights and with the sound of salsa music pulsing from it.

"Hey, Mick, glad you and Rachel could make it," Hector called out. "Welcome to Latin Transylvania."

Hector wore a traditional Cuban *guayabera*, a white cotton shirt with four patch pockets on the front and *alforza* pleats running vertically, worn untucked over black pants. His hair was done in a fake widow's peak and he wore fake long sideburns and vampire fangs.

Hector crossed the entryway to greet Mickey and Rachel. He introduced them to his mother-in-law, Serena, the woman handing out candy at the door, and his mother, Consuela. Then he said, "Come in, please. I'll take you out to the bar for something to drink." He walked them through the house. Before the back steps, Hector turned and said, "My family is scattered all around here. I'll introduce you as we run into them."

If the street outside was a scene, Hector's house and backyard were a scene and a half. Animated coffins were everywhere, opening and closing to recorded sounds of creaking wood, ghoulish laughter and hissing noises. Bats swung from the stairway and a life-sized Count Dracula presided from his open coffin on the second-floor landing. The house and backyard were packed with people, half in costume, half of those seemingly Hector's family, all consistent with the Riveras' theme—Latin Transylvania. The men and boys wore outfits matching Hector's and the women wore push up bras under white blouses, streaked hair, fangs and black eye shadow.

The two side gates of the backyard were open to the neighbors' yards, and partiers milled in and out.

Hector walked up to a bar, tended by another Latin vampire. Rachel and Mickey ordered drinks. Mickey smelled a wood fire and the aroma of cooking. He glanced over to see a pig on a spit over a bed of hot coals in the yard.

"Part of the tradition," Hector said. "We Latins love our pork."

Rachel and Mickey mingled, Hector introducing them around, eventually to Maria, Hector's wife. She was a short, slim woman with dark hair and lively brown eyes. "I heard so much about you both," she said, smiling.

Paul arrived with a goddess on his arm that had to be Jennifer. She was cool toward him when they were introduced, but she warmed up after a few minutes. Later, Paul and Mickey stood near the rear steps of the brownstone looking out on the backyard. Mickey watched Rachel and Jennifer talking, both of them smiling and laughing, gesturing with their arms. "She's a beautiful woman," Mickey said.

"Thanks. I agree. And Rachel is wonderful. And I know what else you're thinking. What's Jennifer doing with me? Most girls who look like that—particularly Victoria's Secret models—go out with professional football quarterbacks or rock stars."

Mickey chuckled.

He watched as Rachel walked over to the bar, leaving Jennifer standing by herself. A man Mickey had been introduced to as the young lawyer who lived next door stepped over to Jennifer and spoke to her. After a moment Mickey saw Jennifer's back stiffen and her lips pull tight.

"Oh, man, look at Jennifer," Paul said. "This guy's gotta be using some cheesy lines on her. She *hates* getting hit on. Watch this."

Mickey saw the man cock his head and step closer to her, and then Jennifer barked something right into his face. The man stepped back and Jennifer kept going at him, a few other partiers turning their heads to look. Then Jennifer turned around and walked over to join Rachel at the bar.

"I see what you mean." Mickey filed it away. "How did you meet her?"

"On line at a Starbucks. She looked like she'd just rolled out of bed. She's a down-to-earth girl. We talked about baseball."

A while later Hector and Mickey stood at the front door taking turns handing out candy.

"Great house," Mickey said. "And a great neighborhood."

"My father-in-law's before me. When he died I bought it. It was passed to him by his father, and his grandfather before that."

"You must do all right. I know a lot of investment bankers and Wall Street lawyers that would love a place like this."

Hector shrugged. "Fourth-generation. When Maria's great-grandfather bought it, you could hardly give these houses away. With each generation we mark it to market, but the selling generation takes back a big mortgage. Maybe in a few more generations it will be paid off."

"Sounds like a great deal."

"Yes. At least this way if you miss a payment because your car needs brakes or your kids need braces, some crazy bank doesn't come and foreclose you. All in the family."

"You all live together here?"

"Yes, all except Raquel out in Jersey and Rafael in the Bronx. Four generations on four floors including the basement, all full of Perezes and Riveras. The Latin way." He smiled. "Family. Sometimes my sainted mother-in-law makes me crazy with her bossing, still thinks it's her house. But she's the mother of my Maria, the grandmother of my children and the great grand-mother of my grandchildren. So what can you do but smile?"

By 9 p.m. the flow of trick-or-treaters had dried up to a trickle. Hector waved Mickey to the backyard just as the DJ turned the salsa music on his rig up another 15 decibels.

"Now the real party starts," Hector shouted over the music. He ran out to the patio and started moving to the beat. Maria found him and they started salsa dancing. Couples joined them and the patio became a dance floor. Jennifer and Paul joined in, moving like pros.

Mickey found Rachel again, and the two of them stood beside the patio watching the dancers, Rachel moving her shoulders and hips to the beat. Hector came over a few minutes later and pulled Rachel out onto the dance floor. Mickey was surprised that she didn't resist. Hector was yelling to Rachel over the music, giving her instructions on the dance. He moved next to her and showed her his footwork. She started moving with him, and after a moment he spun and took her hand, wrapped the other arm around her waist, and they started dancing. Mickey was beaming, enjoying seeing the glow on Rachel's cheeks, her smile, her hair moving as Hector guided her around the dance floor.

Mickey felt a tap on the shoulder and turned to see Maria extending her arm out toward the dance floor.

"Oh no, I can't dance," Mickey shouted over the music.

"I tell you a secret. Neither can Hector. But he fakes it so good that even Hector don't know."

She took his hand.

"I guess this means you're not going to let me off the hook."

"I show you how to fake it." A moment later they were out on the floor, Mickey feeling as if his shoelaces were tied together trying to mimic Maria's moves.

After a minute Maria said, "You mind if I lead?"

"If you don't, nobody will."

She started moving around the floor, Mickey actually feeling like he was dancing after a while. He saw Rachel smile at him over Hector's shoulder. When the song ended, Hector came over and whisked Maria away.

"We might as well," Mickey said to Rachel. And as the music started up again they danced. Little vampires appeared with trays of glasses, weaving through the crowd, the dancers taking shots of something from them and throwing them back. Then Manuel, one of Hector's grandchildren that Mickey and Rachel had been introduced to, held out a shot to Mickey. "Patron Platinum. Poppi Hector calls it 'nectar of the gods.'"

What the hell. Mickey took it and drank it.

He looked over to see Rachel's eyes widen and her mouth go agape. Then she reached to Manuel's tray and grabbed a glass, downed it. They started dancing again.

Mickey didn't know how many shots he and Rachel did, but after half an hour he realized he was leading.

Mickey awakened the next morning with no idea where he was. He felt warmth on his arm from the sun streaming in the window. His head was throbbing, his stomach was in torment and his mouth tasted like rotted lemons. Then he remembered.

Tequila.

Rachel doing shots with him out on the dance floor. He must be in a bedroom upstairs at Hector's. At least he hoped so.

He sat up in bed, realizing he was naked. Then he saw another shape under the covers. *Uh-oh.* He turned to see Rachel next to him, still sleeping.

He couldn't remember how they got here, anything after the dance floor. But here they were, together in bed, so something must've happened.

Then he got a panicked thought: what if she remembered and he didn't? Would that insult her? Then another: what if nothing happened, but she didn't remember and thought something had?

He knew her well enough to know that the simple fact they were here wouldn't sit well with her. Sleeping with another man when she was engaged to someone else wasn't something Marvin Feldman's daughter did. Even if the man she'd slept with was her ex-husband. Somehow Mickey didn't think her statement of the night before, "I'm a grown woman," contemplated this.

Get out of here. Now.

He'd sneak out, go downstairs, and when he saw Rachel later he'd act like nothing happened. He inched his way out from under the covers and slid to a sitting position on the bed, his pulse elevated, making the throbbing in his temples torture.

Rachel stirred.

Mickey froze. He thought for a moment he'd throw up.

She let out a long sigh, then stopped moving. He looked around and saw his clothes scattered on a chair across the room.

He stood up, gently, so as not to jostle the bed, and started tiptoeing across the room to the chair.

Rachel stirred again.

Mickey stopped.

She rolled over to face him, but with her eyes still closed.

He felt a flash of alarm and decided to make a break for it. He crossed the last 10 feet in three long steps and ran into the chair, stubbing his toe and slamming his knee. As he caught himself with his hands on the seat of the chair he heard the rustle of the covers from behind him. He couldn't tell which hurt more, his toe, his knee or his head.

"Mickey!" Rachel called out.

He spun around.

"Mickey! You're naked!"

For a moment he had the absurd notion to cross his hands over his genitals. Rachel was sitting up in the bed, her eyes sleepy but wide open, her face showing alarm. Mickey's gaze instinctively went to her naked breasts.

At that, she looked down at her chest. "Oh my God!" she said and pulled the sheets up to cover herself.

Mickey now decided his best course of action was to appear as nonchalant as possible. He turned back around to pick up his clothes. "I'm just going to get dressed, and then I'll leave to give you some privacy so you can get up."

"Did anything happen? I mean, did we . . . ?"

Mickey turned to face her again. "Do you really want me to answer that?"

"I wouldn't have asked you if I didn't."

Oh, what the hell. "To be honest, I have no idea. The last thing I remember was us dancing and doing shots of tequila."

He heard Rachel sigh.

"But based on the evidence—you and me naked in bed, and hardly strangers to each other in that venue—I'd say we must have had a good time." He smiled.

"I'm having trouble finding any humor in this."

"Come on, Rachel, you have to admit it's kind of funny, the two of us getting stinko blotto and then picking up where we left off as an old married couple."

"You're suggesting that I was unfaithful to Walter, my fiancé."

"But neither of us remembers, so did it happen at all? It's kind of like that old saying, something like, If a tree falls in the forest and nobody sees it, did it fall?" He held out his arms and grinned.

"For God's sake, Mickey, please put some clothes on!"

"I'll be out of here in a minute." He turned around and started putting on his clothes. When he finished, he said, "I'll see you downstairs," and left.

———◇———

Despite what Rachel had said, as Mickey left the room, he still found the humor in the situation. By the time he got downstairs, thinking more about the look on Rachel's face, he didn't. When he walked into the kitchen, only Maria and Hector were there. Hector raised an eyebrow and patted the stool next to him. Maria, standing behind Hector, said, "Coffee?"

Even the word made Mickey's head feel better. "Please."

She poured a cup and pushed it to him across the island.

"You did okay on the dance floor, my friend," Hector said. "We'll make a Latin out of you yet."

Maria looked Mickey in the eye from behind Hector. She made a face, as if to say, "Forget it," and rolled her eyes. Mickey smiled back at her and put his hands around the mug of coffee, feeling its warmth.

"You want eggs or something?" Hector asked. "Consuelo can make you something. I need to leave shortly. My shift starts in an hour and a half."

"Anything," Mickey said.

"How about a cheese omelet?" Hector said. He turned to look at Maria. "We got cheese in the downstairs fridge, don't we, hon?"

Maria looked at him as if confused for a moment, then said, "Oh yes. The cheese in the basement fridge." She left the kitchen.

Hector turned back to Mickey and said, "You were on a roll last night. I was rooting for you." He grinned. "And I think you did okay, you stud."

Mickey felt some college-boy bravado again, then reminded himself he didn't remember anything, and any thought of telling his buddy about his triumph of the night before went out the window. "The sad thing is, if I did get lucky I can't even recall it. When she comes downstairs, please act like nothing happened."

Hector nodded. "Rachel and you are a nice couple."

"*Were* a nice couple."

"Last night you two looked pretty tight."

"Yes and no. It didn't go so well after she woke up."

"Yes, but she's still here, and so are you."

"We'll see," Mickey said. He heard Rachel's voice in the hallway talking to Maria. He felt his shoulders sag as he realized that Rachel was making her apologies, thanking Consuelo and saying good-bye.

Hector apparently heard it, too, and gave Mickey a look with his eyebrows raised. Mickey heard the front door close, and then Maria walked back into the kitchen.

"No cheese," Maria said.

Mickey reached the front door and opened it as Rachel was descending the front steps.

"Rachel, wait."

She turned and said, "I'm so mortified. I made my apologies to Maria, but I'm afraid the Riveras must think I'm some frivolous New York socialite who can't handle her liquor and doesn't know how to behave at a party."

"Don't be ridiculous. These are real people and they enjoyed your company." Mickey's mind was working, trying to figure out where her head was, how he could do some damage control, because he knew Rachel was at least halfway unhinged.

She paused and held his gaze for a long moment before she responded. Finally she said, "I don't think this has been a good idea."

Another long pause.

"What hasn't?" Mickey said.

"I think you know what I mean. You and me spending time together, even at times acting as if nothing has . . . gone on . . ." Her voice trailed off.

"Gone on?"

"Changed in our lives. Your scandal, our divorce." She paused. "Look, I'm happy to help you, and I'd do it again. I feel that it's my obligation. You know we've shared so much, Mickey." Her voice broke. "But that's all in the past now. And we haven't been acting as if it is. And I'm not blaming you. I know that last night I wasn't acting as if it was in the past, either."

Mickey didn't respond, waiting.

Rachel said, "Last night I asked you why. You know I've always wondered why you haven't asked me why."

"Why about what?"

"Why I divorced you."

"I always figured it was the practical side of you. It was the only thing to do to preserve our—your—way of life."

Mickey realized his breathing had become labored. He waited for her to respond and then realized she was crying. He stepped toward her to hold her but she backed away.

She said, "I'm still ashamed of myself. I think I'm weak. I wasn't always this way. I don't know what happened, but I'm sorry, Mickey."

"There's no reason to apologize."

"Yes, there is. I'm not really sure what I'm doing. All I know right now is that this has been a mistake. And what we did last night—"

"Rachel, I'm not sure that anything happened—"

"A woman knows."

Mickey paused, not sure how to respond.

Rachel said, "It happened." Her voice was choked with emotion. "So I don't think we should see each other anymore. I don't think trying to be friends at this point is rational."

Mickey felt pressure in his chest, as if someone were pushing him against a wall.

Rachel said, "I care for you, Mickey. More than just care for you. You know that. And I'll always be here to help you if it really gets bad for you." And then she whispered, "But we need to say good-bye," and turned to walk into the street. He watched her hail a cab and get in, then watched it drive off.

Mickey felt a pinprick, and then the sensation spread throughout his chest. He remembered that feeling from a long, long time ago, from before he'd started dating Rachel, maybe back in college, or was it high school? A broken heart.

CHAPTER 4

When the crate from Bouchard containing the painting arrived via UPS a few days later, Paul was up at the Met studying again. Mickey waited for Paul to return before pulling out a hammer and screwdriver to pry open the protective wooden case inside the cardboard shipping box. He got the top off and reached inside, ready to slide out the painting while Paul supported the box.

"Ready?" Mickey asked. He slid it out of the box.

"Wow," Paul said. "The grays in the sky are even more menacing and the thick gobs of paint and rough brushstrokes even more pronounced than *Women Mending Nets in the Dunes.*"

"Quit showing off."

Mickey stood the painting up on the sofa and stepped back from it.

"It's smaller than I thought," Paul said.

"It's 13.5 by 20 inches. Exactly the size of the original."

"Do you think it'll pass?"

"How would I know? The only way to tell is when we get our expert appraiser over here to authenticate it. Bouchard gave me the names of three of them and the one I liked best should be here later." Mickey leaned in close to the painting, drew a deep breath through his nose, then stood back and nodded. "The only thing I can comment on is that there's no odor of linseed oil. Bouchard told me that was a deal killer on a painting that's supposed to be this old. He said he adds special driers to the paints, uses a hair dryer between coats, then leaves the windows open for a few weeks to let it finish gassing off."

Paul walked over to the sofa, leaned over to put his own nose to the painting and sniffed. He turned back to Mickey and said, "Smells like dust. No, a Bordeaux that's turned."

I've created a monster.

The appraiser, Byron Scopes, an art history professor at NYU, arrived a few hours later. Mickey and Paul waited an eternity after the front desk called upstairs to say the man was here. Finally Paul said, "I'm gonna see if something happened to the guy." Paul opened the door to see a little man wearing a tweed suit standing in the doorway, holding a briefcase in one hand and an artist's folio in the other. "Oh," Paul said, startled. Then he straightened his back and said, "I'm Paul Hilton. Welcome. I presume you're—"

"Scopes," the man said, almost inaudibly. Paul waved him in and closed the door. Once inside, Scopes said, "I knocked, but softly. I always try to handle these matters with complete discretion."

Mickey saw Paul stifling a laugh.

"May I?" Scopes said, now in a normal tone, pointing to the coffee table and holding out his briefcase. Paul nodded and the man put his briefcase down, then his folio. He removed his suit jacket and took his time folding it and placing it on a chair. Then he opened his briefcase and removed a magnifying glass, a microscope, a box of latex gloves and another odd device that Mickey couldn't identify that looked like an old-fashioned tube radio with the guts exposed.

Scopes stepped forward and started to perform his examination, first with the magnifying glass, then with the microscope, finally with the odd-looking radio-like machine. After he finished using that device, he turned and said, "A portable spectrometer."

"I know," Paul said, standing with his chin raised, observing over Scopes' shoulder. "And a nice one, too."

Mickey shot Paul a look.

Next Scopes removed a print of *View of the Sea* from the artist's folio and set it face up on the coffee table. Then he took a blank whiteboard out and stood it up next to the painting on the sofa. He removed yet another mechanism from his briefcase and set it on top of the print on the coffee table. He plugged it in and the image of the original print of *View of the Sea* appeared on the whiteboard next to the painting, with crosshatched lines on it. It was the same kind of projector device that Bouchard had used as he was copying the painting. Scopes pulled out another projector, set it on the coffee table, and turned it on. Crosshatched lines appeared on the painting. He took about five minutes to adjust both projectors until the grids were aligned perfectly on both the projected print and the painting.

Mickey felt his heart rate pick up as Scopes approached the painting again with his magnifying glass. He peered for a long moment over his pointed nose at the red flag on the boat in the middle of the painting. Then he went back over to the projection of his print and did the same. The man showed no reaction. He kept on for half an hour, working methodically, looking at dozens of grids on the painting, then the print.

Mickey's calves and shoulders felt tight from having his body tensed. When Scopes started to sigh as he looked at the grids, Mickey began to lose hope. Bouchard had a reputation as being the best, but you never knew with these things.

Scopes turned from the painting and said, "May I touch the painting to confirm something?"

Paul stepped forward with the authority of ownership and said, "Confirm what?"

"The presence of grains of sand from Scheveningen in the lower right quadrant of the painting."

Paul nodded his consent.

Mickey closed his eyes for a moment. When he opened them Scopes had raised a gloved hand. He ran his finger over the surface of the painting. One spot, then two more. Finally he turned and said, "It's genuine, a treasure."

Mickey let out his breath as inconspicuously as he could.

Scopes smiled for the first time, almost the first expression he'd shown since entering the room. "I feel privileged to have been able to evaluate it." He turned and began putting his instruments back in his briefcase, then slid the print back into his folio. He put his coat back on and stood in front of the coffee table to regard the painting for a few moments. Then he turned and looked first at Paul, then Mickey. "To whom shall I present my bill?"

Paul opened his palm toward Mickey. "Mr. Steinberg is my agent," he said and sat down.

Mickey smiled and said, "That's right, I'll take it. I assume cash is fine."

After he closed the door behind Scopes, Mickey turned to Paul and held his finger to his lips. He waited about 30 seconds, then opened the door a crack. He closed the door again and said, "Okay, he's gone."

Paul bounded across the room and shook Mickey's hand so hard he almost knocked him over. "Man alive! I thought I was gonna shit my pants."

"Let's break out a bottle of champagne."

The next day, Mickey and Paul sat beside each other at the coffee table in their room at the Chelsea, making final plans. They'd called Bouchard out at Yankton and were waiting to hear back from him to set their final strategy. Mickey said, "Once we get our process rolling, the buyers should come to us. Most markets are pretty efficient, in part because people can't keep their mouths shut."

Mickey said it with his normal self-assurance, wanting to make sure Paul quit worrying—for the last 48 hours he'd been peppering Mickey with questions reflecting his doubts about their ability to pull off the deal: "You're still sure somebody's gonna pay this kind of scratch for a painting, huh? You really think there's a big enough group of buyers to get a hot auction going here? You think getting an expert to certify the painting will convince the buyers?"

Mickey figured it was natural; stage fright before opening night, and Paul would be at center stage for this deal. At the same time, Mickey wondered about the field of buyers himself. He'd spent the last few days going through his contacts, mining those he knew who were major art collectors. He was sure his summary message was enough to tantalize many of them to call back, even despite the fact he'd been jailed for insider trading. But he didn't know how many.

He put down his list on the coffee table in front of Paul.

"You'll recognize some of these names."

Paul looked at the list. "Wow, man," he said. "Murdoch, Geffen, Gates, Buffett, Wynn."

"These guys are billionaires. Twenty million for a painting is popcorn money to them."

"Yeah, but if they find out we're screwing them they'll have our hearts cut out."

Mickey was beginning to get tired of reassuring Paul. But he forced himself to stay calm, blinking his eyes, thinking about how bad it would be to send Paul out there operating at less than 100% bravado.

Bouchard called back. Mickey put him on speaker.

"We're ready to start calling buyers, but wanted to touch base with you one more time before we do to get any final pointers on unique aspects to an art sale like this."

"Excellent. Gentlemen, we are on the eve of an exciting and momentous series of events."

Mickey imagined Bouchard holding a finger aloft, gesturing like a Shakespearean actor, his smiling eyes upturned. Mickey smiled at Paul. "Walk us through how you see the process unfolding," he said.

Bouchard said, "We'll employ the same process that is used by most private sellers of legitimate art—used in hundreds of major and thousands of minor transactions each year. In our case, the proposed sale of this lost masterpiece should draw all serious collectors into our process, creating a frothy bidding environment unprecedented in recent years. Now that our expert has authenticated the painting, he will speak with experts that other buyers customarily employ. It is a small network. In most cases, the experts work for multiple buyers—an accepted practice in the fraternity of buyers of these rare treasures."

Mickey said, "That will create leaks all over the place."

"Exactly. As a consequence, many of the buyers will contact you before you reach them. But as I said, the network of these buyers and experts is small, so that by the time word leaks out to Interpol or the FBI about a stolen painting being sold, the transaction will be completed and everybody will have vanished, or if questioned by the authorities, will adhere to the code of silence that prevails in this cultured world of refined aesthetes. Once we have decided on the field of potential bidders, then we arrange viewings of the painting for the buyers and their experts, and meetings with Paul, our young connoisseur of art. All of this must be accomplished in a short time frame."

Paul said, "Sounds like a three-ring circus."

Mickey said, "It's no different than selling a high technology company that everybody's clamoring to get their hands on. Get the deal all lined up, then leak it to some blabbermouth research analyst who'll splash it all over the industry. Deny it consistently until the last minute so the buyers think you're shutting them out for your preferred players. Then sit back and watch the drama as the buyers fall all over themselves to get in on the action. See them stretch beyond any reasonable limits on price because they can't stand the thought of losing the bid to one of the other players they know must be in the hunt. Only in this case there are no lawyers, no contracts and it's a cash deal."

"And no taxes to pay," Paul said, grinning.

Bouchard continued. "It will be important to establish Paul's credibility as well as the painting's. Critical, in fact."

Mickey nodded his understanding.

Bouchard said, "Most of the members of this beau monde cadre of collectors know each other. As such, they know their transactions are within their class, safe from pedestrians who might brag about how they rubbed elbows with the elite, ultimately sending the authorities knocking. Sellers unknown to them must first pass the hurdle of credibility in order to be taken seriously and judged safe to conduct business with. Naturally, Mickey, your relationships with many of these buyers will go a long way toward that. But unless our young collector, Mr. Paul Hilton, can establish his knowledge and love of art of this rarified quality, and the lifestyle that evidences the means to possess it, our buyers will shun him, regardless of how tantalizing the prize he's offering for sale. Aside from the concern about loose lips, they may suspect him to be working a con, trying to conduct a sting for the authorities, or even seeking to initiate a publicity scandal at their expense. In 1976, one such seller went so far as to attempt to blackmail the Hunt family, threatening to disclose that one of the brothers bought a stolen Dalí from him unless they paid him millions in additional hush money."

Mickey saw Paul taking it in.

"So as we say in French, '*Regardez attentivement,*' young Paul. 'Look sharp.'"

After they got off the phone with Bouchard, Mickey started calling buyers. He'd made calls to about half of them when his phone rang. He looked at the caller ID and felt a rush of energy. This man wouldn't bother to call back unless he was interested. "You'll get your chance to find out if Buffett's a buyer right now." Mickey hit ANSWER and put the phone to his ear. "Thanks for calling back. How are you?"

"Fine, just fine, Mickey. That was an interesting call to get. You haven't lost your touch for the teaser deal summary."

"You're one of the first people I thought of when I came across this."

"Right," Buffett laughed. "Pardon my asking, but when did you get into this business?"

"You know my situation. So I've transitioned into a new line of work. Unusual deals. Hard-to-find items that people on my Rolodex, like you, will find interesting."

"Your message said 19th-century impressionism. Bold swatches of paint with untamed brushstrokes consistent with some of the other paintings in my collection. So what are we talking about here?"

"Vincent, early. 1882."

Buffett didn't respond immediately. Mickey figured he was flipping through imaginary prints in his mind, trying to identify which one it might be. "What price range are you thinking?"

"Come on. This will be like any other auction. Highest bidder takes it, but I don't think you'll see it go for less than $30 million."

"Where might I have seen this last?"

"Amsterdam, no later than 2002."

"I have a particular fondness for seascapes."

"I've heard that."

"This is a coincidence. I happen to have recently spoken to Christie's about selling a van Gogh from the same period, a lesser work I can live without."

"Oh?"

"*Women Mending Nets in the Dunes.* If you know anyone who'd be interested, please let me know." Buffett went on for a few minutes with the details about his painting, then came back to the business at hand. "Now about your client's painting. When can my man and I see it?"

"Next week."

After Mickey hung up, Paul said, "Well shut my mouth. I only heard your side of it, but I guess I'm a believer."

"You guess?" Mickey smiled. He picked up the phone and called Carlos Slim, the richest man in Mexico, priming him on the deal for ten minutes.

Two hours later, Mickey had seven potential buyers lined up, with five others he'd yet to hear back from. Only two prospects had said they weren't interested.

Mickey figured they needed to get out of the hotel room because Paul had started pacing. He imagined Paul turning over in his mind the fact that he'd be meeting these industry titans in the next few days, passing himself off as their equals in the art collecting world.

Mickey said, "Let's go out and have a relaxing dinner tonight. We'll splurge."

They ate at Le Bernardin. Paul did himself proud discussing red burgundies with the sommelier that would go with the poached skate he ordered, as well as Mickey's wild striped bass. He wanted a wine with major age so it wouldn't overpower the fish. The sommelier seemed genuinely impressed when Paul settled on a Dujac Charmes-Chambertin, 1978.

When they returned home to their room at the Chelsea, Mickey's cell phone rang again.

"Hello, Mickey, it's Walter Goldstein."

His voice was as oily as ever. "Walter. How are you?"

"Intrigued."

For a moment Mickey wondered if Goldstein was talking about Rachel and him on Halloween night at Hector's house. Then he realized that was silly; Rachel would never say anything to Goldstein about that. He had to be calling about the van Gogh. "I thought that might be your reaction."

"Yes. So how do we proceed?"

"Are you a buyer, or acting as an intermediary?"

"Consider me a buyer."

"I assume you're aware of the general price range a unique asset like this will command."

Goldstein let out a snort. "I rather think my experience with what unique assets of this nature fetch in the marketplace is considerably deeper than yours."

"Viewings will begin next week. After that we'll move quickly. Will you be using an appraiser or representing yourself?"

Goldstein chuckled. Mickey imagined him with that insinuating smile, bordering on a leer. "I'm representing myself, of course."

A fool for a client. "I'll let you know." Mickey couldn't resist a little jab to let Goldstein know he'd been spending time with Rachel. "Are you back? Rachel told me you were in Europe."

A pause. Then Goldstein said in a lowered voice, "Why of course, old man. I'm at home in our apartment right now."

"Our apartment." Touché. Round to Goldstein on an uppercut just before the bell. But Mickey knew this was a long contest. He hung up, smiled at Paul and said, "This is going better than I'd expected."

Word travels fast. Goldstein had obviously been tipped off about the van Gogh by one of the experts. Yes, this shadow network of buyers of stolen art was very efficient.

Then Mickey had a thought that took some of the air out of him: the fact that the process leaked meant that nobody was to be trusted. Paul and he needed to be more than careful, even paranoid.

Moravian White walked past the Jew dry cleaners on Rockaway Parkway down the street from Yummy Yummy, just to see what was going on, a dark blue hoodie on him, the hood pulled over his head and face as far as he could. There was no police black-and-white or dark green Crown Vic outside, and no bozos standing on the corners watching, pretending to be locals but with shined shoes giving them away as cops. Seemed like they were here every day on and off, but no permanent stakeout. He still wasn't going up to his apartment, but just wanted to see for himself how close they were watching it.

It was like at work, where they stopped in a few times a day at Foremost Carburetor to check up, see if he showed. Rohit Kahn letting him know how many times and when, usually the same two guys in the green Crown Vic, Rohit telling them Moravian was still on vacation, maybe with relatives in Jamaica. He was on vacation, so it wasn't a lie, Randy Jolson, the boss at Foremost, letting him take his two weeks with pay on account of 23 years service at Foremost, Randy a good man, fair and honest. But not so honest with the cops; he agreed with Rohit's cover story for Moravian, and let Moravian stay at his daughter's apartment over on First Avenue while she was away at a friend's in New Rochelle studying for her CPA exam.

Moravian turned around and walked into the alley next to the dry cleaners, thinking. He knew this wouldn't last forever. He'd need to figure out where to go long term, think through how to get himself back into his life again, his job, his apartment. After he found Steinberg and did him. Not yet, though. After.

He knew Bucky Pierson was looking for him, Rohit telling him, Splits Duncan telling him, too. Moravian knew Bucky was looking for him because Jack Grass wanted to know what was going on with Steinberg, Jack still thinking Moravian was doing it for the money, not because of Steinberg sending Dontelle to jail. Moravian didn't care about Jack now. Jack could wait.

He looked up and down Rockaway Parkway, checking again for the green Crown Vic, then headed toward the L train back to

Manhattan. Back to the Steinberg woman's apartment building on Park Avenue. Two white guys who looked like cops always stationed at the building, one of them usually in the car outside, the other in the lobby. What did they think? She'd never go outside the apartment building? Never go to a lunch with her girlfriends? Never go to Bergdorf Goodman to exchange a cashmere sweater?

Moravian laughed. Even if she went all the way across town he could follow her and get her alone again to find out where Steinberg was.

Rich women like that needed Bergdorf's. Or Bloomingdale's. Or Saks. Only a question of time. Eventually he'd find her alone.

And after last time, he'd make sure she told him everything. Then he'd get to Steinberg. Then figure out what came after, but not until then.

"We have a high-quality problem," Mickey said to Paul. He'd just hung up his phone and sat down on the sofa in their room at the Chelsea.

Paul looked down at him and said with his chin raised, "And that high-quality problem would be?"

Mickey looked back up at him, wondering if this was the time to cut Paul down to size. His ego had been getting out of control, Mickey no longer sure that Paul could distinguish between himself and his character as a hotshot art collector. Mickey decided it was the wrong time, reined himself in.

Mickey said, "We have too many buyers. Seventeen. We can't possibly keep them all in the process."

"That's 17 meet-and-greets, 17 viewings. I can handle that."

"If we meet with them all, we'll never keep things under wraps. We've got leaks as it is. Meeting with that many buyers could take a week or two. If we hang around for that long we'll have Interpol or the FBI on our tails."

Paul laughed. "Yeah, but so what? We aren't selling a stolen painting. It's a fake."

Now Mickey was starting to get annoyed. "Yes, it's a fake. So even if we don't get charged for selling stolen property, Interpol or the FBI steps in and nails us for trying to scam people, or simply screws up our whole process. We wind up with no deal. Not only that, but no chance to ever talk to any of these buyers again, because they'll know we were trying to swindle them."

Paul thought for a moment. He said, "I still don't like it. What if we lose some of the big guns, the guys who might've been top bidders?"

"That's a chance you always have to take. We just need to think it through, be intelligent about it."

Paul still wasn't giving up. "What if we do a blitz of meetings? Breakfast, lunch and dinner, get through them all in less than a week?"

"There's too much room for a slipup. These men know the art world. You mistakenly refer to a van Gogh painting as a Monet and not only do we lose that buyer, but his expert tells the other experts, he tells the other buyers, the whole process comes crashing down."

"I know the art, too."

"You've been cramming it for weeks. These guys have lived it for decades, buying it, selling it."

Paul paused, seemed to be thinking.

Mickey added, "And don't forget who these people are. These men will certainly want to know who they're doing business with, check you out."

"Yeah, man, but we've got a good cover story. I made my money because my father was an early investor in one of George Soros' hedge funds, then I doubled down on that investment after my father died, I've been living in Hong Kong—"

"I know your backstory," Mickey cut him off, getting tired of this. "I wrote it, remember?"

Paul gave Mickey a wounded look. Or was it indignant? Mickey realized it was a delicate balance. Keeping Paul from getting increasingly out of control so he wouldn't say something stupid at the wrong moment, but at the same time wanting him to be full of bravado, even cocky when he met with the buyers.

Mickey added, "Finally, we can't afford it. Seventeen buyers is too many hotel rooms, dinners, limos, and such to set up our process. We've only got about $16 thousand or so left of the money Rachel lent me, and we haven't even started yet."

Paul said, "Okay. So what do we do?"

"We change the process into a two-stage auction. We ask for first-round, preliminary bids, what the buyers would pay assuming they verify the painting as genuine. We cut the group of buyers down to size based on the best bids we receive. Then we do our second round, a reduced number of meet-and-greets and viewings before we ask for final bids."

"But how can they do the first-round bid at all if they haven't even seen the painting yet?"

"That's where our expert appraiser comes in. Our man talks to their experts—and remember, their experts may be working for multiple buyers—and gives them his assurance. Their experts will have an opportunity to verify the painting in the viewing just prior to the final bids."

Paul seemed to have stopped listening. He was looking in the corner at the crate containing the painting, thinking. Then he turned back to Mickey. "You've lost confidence in me being able to pull off the meet-and-greets, haven't you?"

So it was *a wounded look earlier.* Mickey smiled at him. "No, not at all. We just need to manage this thing correctly to avoid shooting ourselves in the foot."

Paul nodded. "Okay. So what's next?"

"I call our expert and the buyers and tell them the game plan has changed."

"You think any will drop out of the process as a result?"

"We'll see."

Mickey picked up the phone and called their expert, Byron Scopes, and filled him in, then started calling buyers. About ten minutes after speaking to Scopes, Mickey was talking to one of the buyers when he heard his phone beep with an incoming call. He looked at the screen: *Goldstein.* Mickey decided to let him wait; the more anxious a buyer was, the more anxious he'd become if you strung him out.

Paul started pacing. Mickey, still on the phone, gave him a look and Paul whispered, "I'm going out for a walk." Mickey sighed, relieved.

About ten minutes later during another buyer call, Mickey's phone beeped with another incoming call. He checked: Goldstein again. He smiled and went back to his conversation.

After another hour he'd finished all his outbound calls and was waiting for some of the buyers to call him back. He set his phone down and leaned back to relax, then heard the clink of an incoming text message. He picked up the phone and saw on the screen: MUST SPEAK TO YOU. URGENT. *Goldstein again.* Mickey smiled.

He let Goldstein stew for another half hour and then called him back.

"Mickey, good of you to call back, old man."

"What's on your mind?"

Goldstein paused, cleared his throat, paused again. It sounded to Mickey as if he was having trouble deciding what he was going to say. Mickey didn't want to make it easier for him, so he just waited.

Eventually Goldstein said, "I wanted to have a confidential conversation with you about preempting your process."

"Go on," Mickey said. It was something Mickey believed was possible, since it happened once in a while in auction processes to sell companies, but he'd never considered that Goldstein possessed either the wherewithal or the chutzpah to pull it off.

Goldstein said, "I'll offer you a price sufficiently above what you might ever expect any rational buyer to pay, and you shut down your auction process so we can do a deal."

Mickey waited for him to go on. When he didn't, Mickey said, "That's it?"

"Well, I should think my statement would be rather dispositive, don't you?"

"Not necessarily. To even consider disrupting, let alone shutting down our process, you'd need to show us such a blowaway price that you'd shock my prior expectations of your limited ability to compete with the other buyers in this process." After a pause he added, "No offense intended, Walter."

Goldstein exhaled as if annoyed. "And how might I go about that?"

"You have me on the phone. I'm listening." Mickey tried to resist the antsy feeling in his chest about what would come next. He had to admit he was at least curious.

Goldstein said, "I propose that I have the opportunity to meet with your seller to see that he isn't some poseur before I am allowed a private viewing to assess the genuineness of the painting."

"I've already told you we aren't giving anyone that opportunity on an exclusive basis. There's no advantage to us to do that. In fact I've just been calling all the buyers to let them know that we're revising our process into a two-stage auction, because we have too many parties involved—"

"But—" Goldstein tried to cut in.

Mickey talked over him "—and we need to narrow the field. Consider yourself on notice to that effect as of now. We'll let you know when first-round indications of interest will be due. You'll have an opportunity to first speak with our own expert to get his opinion that the painting is genuine. Then you'll have a chance to throw us one number. One shot, that's it. And then we'll decide who makes the second round."

Mickey paused, waiting.

"How about we cut through all this mishmash, old man. I'm thinking of $40 million."

Mickey smiled so broadly he was afraid to say anything, for fear Goldstein might hear it in his voice. He grabbed the edge of the table to help keep from laughing. Finally he said, "Should I consider that your first-round indication?"

Goldstein let out his breath. "*View of the Sea* is a great masterpiece, but only an uninitiated fool could walk away from a price of that magnitude." Goldstein waited a moment, and then added, "No offense intended, old man."

"I'll speak to my client," Mickey said.

"Yes, do that. But I caution you not to take too long. If I'm disappointed by the response, I may choose to withdraw from the process entirely. This nonsense of two-stage chicanery has taken all the enjoyment out of a business that was once conducted pleasurably between gentlemen."

Before Mickey could respond, Goldstein hung up.

Well I'll be.

———◇———

Mickey was seated at a table in the Campbell Apartment in Grand Central Terminal, waiting for Goldstein, Jennifer and Paul to show up for cocktails. He'd negotiated the meeting with Goldstein as if he were setting the stage for a multibillion-dollar merger.

Goldstein said dinner.

Mickey said no, cocktails, and just one at that.

Goldstein said alright, 7:00 p.m.

Mickey said four o'clock.

Goldstein said Wednesday.

Mickey said tomorrow.

Goldstein said the seller and him one-on-one.

Mickey said absolutely not. Mickey would attend or no meeting. And the client's girlfriend. He didn't go anyplace without her when he was in the States.

Goldstein said they'd agree on price.

Mickey said that was out-of-bounds. The client's girlfriend knew nothing about the deal. No reference to it. A pure meet-and-greet, to look each other in the eye.

Goldstein said, alright, cocktails, then, at 4:00 p.m. today at the Front Bar at the Four Seasons restaurant.

Mickey said that was too public. At a quiet spot nobody even knew about.

It'd taken fifteen minutes to hash it out. Mickey's goal was to infuriate Goldstein, make him feel excluded, as if he wasn't worthy, all calculated to make him all the more eager to show that he was. Stomp on the egomaniac's ego until his ego caused him to do something completely irrational. Like actually paying $40 million for a fake van Gogh.

It was Mickey's idea to have Jennifer join them.

"You sure that's a good idea?" Paul had said, his eyebrows raised.

"Have you ever played poker?"

"Some."

"They call her a shill. Usually it's a knockout waitress serving drinks. Or if it's roulette, she'll be seated at the wheel most of the night. She's always working for the house, and she's there to keep the other players in the game, and at the same time break their concentration."

Paul didn't seem convinced, or had something else on his mind he was reluctant to say.

Mickey went on. "Discussion of the deal is off-limits. It'll just be us having a quiet drink with an interesting man I wanted you to meet. And of course we invited your girlfriend to join us. Very low-key, innocent. So you won't have to worry about raising questions in Jennifer's mind."

After a moment Paul gave Mickey a sheepish smile and said, "Jennifer won't do it."

"Why not?"

"Remember Hector's Halloween party?"

Mickey felt a reminder in his stomach of the aftereffects of tequila the next morning. Then a wave of anguish remembering his last conversation with Rachel. "How could I forget?"

"Well, on the way out there, Jennifer really pushed me, man. And I told her."

"Told her?"

"Told her what we were up to."

"Everything?"

"Yeah." Paul lowered his gaze to the floor, his equivalent of hanging his head in shame. "Jennifer told me that if we went forward with this thing, she'd blow the roof off it."

Mickey forced himself not to show any reaction, as when his opponent across the negotiating table dropped a bomb that he hadn't seen coming. He sat, reeling, trying to collect his thoughts, blinking, then nodding slowly. *What a dope this Paul can be.* He couldn't believe it. *All this planning, all this effort.* After a few moments he couldn't help but smile. He'd wanted a talker, and he'd gotten one. "We'll deal with it," he said, still thinking. He realized it was a setback, but all deals had unexpected complications that required you to make adjustments. So why should this deal be any different?

Paul went on. "She said she wouldn't stand for me going back to jail, me this guy who was too gullible to doubt people, and you some high-end Wall Street crook who could talk anybody into anything."

Mickey let it sink in. He knew that's what people probably thought of him, but he hadn't heard it in a direct quote from a twenty-something young woman. It hurt. Mickey said, "So why did you wait until now to tell me this?"

"I thought I could convince her." Now Paul actually hung his head. He looked up again at Mickey and said, "You think this might blow the deal?"

Mickey was thinking on the fly, figuring it out. He said, "Why don't you just ask her if she's willing to play along on meeting for cocktails with Goldstein?"

Paul gave Mickey a look as if he were in pain. Then he said, "She might do it if I tell her the three of us will have a sit-down and talk everything through."

Mickey thought for a moment, imagining Paul telling Jennifer about the deal. Maybe she backed him into a corner and he blurted it out to take the pressure off; maybe he just felt guilty keeping it from her. However it happened, he didn't position it the way Mickey would if he got the chance to pitch it to Jennifer. Mickey said, "Great idea. The two of us can walk her through it together right after cocktails with Goldstein, get her comfortable."

Paul's face brightened.

Now sitting there sipping a Perrier with lime, Mickey was still chewing on it in his mind. *This can work.* He knew Goldstein. And he'd seen Jennifer in action. In fact, he was counting on her behaving in character.

Mickey looked around the Campbell Apartment. The place was designed in 13th-century Florentine style, a 30-by-60-foot single room with a 25-foot-high, beamed ceiling, dark paneling, a massive fireplace at one end and a single glass chandelier in the center. An entrepreneur named John W. Campbell had leased it in the 1920s as an office—used until the late 1940s—because it was the biggest ground-floor room in New York.

Located just off the West Balcony in the southwest corner of Grand Central Terminal, today it was a cocktail lounge, its doorway tucked away inconspicuously just inside the Vanderbilt Avenue entrance to Grand Central. Mickey decided it was the perfect place for a discreet meeting.

Mickey told Paul to bring Jennifer at about 4:30, because he knew Goldstein was too self-important to be on time at 4:00.

Paul watched Jennifer slide a napkin back and forth on the bar at Michael Jordan's on the West Balcony in Grand Central Terminal, an untouched glass of wine in front of her.

She turned to him and asked, "Shouldn't we go over?"

"Not yet. Mickey wants a few minutes alone with the guy."

Jennifer just nodded.

Not much energy. But at least he'd gotten her here. *So far so good.*

His conversation with her to set it up could've gone either way.

He'd greeted her with his best boyish grin when she'd entered her apartment after a shoot. "Mickey's invited you to join us for cocktails with that big art dealer, Goldstein, on our deal. It'll be my first chance to shine."

She narrowed her eyes at him. "Why would I do that?"

"Come on. Cocktails at the Campbell Apartment. The genuine old New York."

"You've got to be joking. You know where I stand on this crazy deal. Now you want to recruit me into it?"

"Babe. It's a *drink*." This was going south fast.

But she hadn't shut him down.

"Besides," she said, "what do you need me for?"

"You complete the picture of the jet-setting young couple. Paul the billionaire art collector with the beautiful, brainy better half."

"What do these men care who they buy from? A priceless work of art speaks for itself."

"Not if the guy who's hawking it smells like a swamp."

"Count me out."

"But babe, Mickey already set it up. It's my fault; we got our wires crossed. When I told him I hadn't talked to you yet, he asked me to apologize to you on his behalf for putting you in this position, but canceling with Goldstein at the last minute could put our whole deal at risk. Once we—"

"Do you think I care about Mickey's deal?" She didn't wait for an answer. "Honey, I care about you, and he's using you."

"I told him that's how you feel. He said right after we get through the Goldstein meeting, the three of us will have a sit-down and hash everything out. Full disclosure."

Jennifer didn't respond, her face stony. But he thought she might be considering it.

"If this guy Goldstein turns out to be a bore, it's only cocktails—we can suffer through that. Then we have a chat with Mickey. Then just you and me out on the town for the night. We can have dinner and go clubbing. Or just come back here, order in Chinese and watch a movie. Anything you want."

She sighed and shook her head at him like he was a goofy little kid.

"Just work with me on this one meeting, please, babe. If we pull off this deal, I'll be set. *You* and I will be set."

"You don't even know Mickey's real agenda. He's a shark and he'll eat you alive."

Paul's muscles tensed, realizing that if he didn't push her over that last step right now, she'd shut him down on the subject for good. "If you still think the deal stinks after our sit-down with Mickey, I'll back out."

That sold it. Jennifer's face softened. "You mean that?"

Paul felt a tremor of discomfort but smiled. "Absolutely." He stepped to her and took her in his arms.

"If we have our meeting with Mickey afterward, okay." She kissed him. Then she lowered her chin. "But if you're even going to pull off cocktails with this guy, we've got work to do."

Now Paul looked over at Jennifer, still sliding the napkin back and forth on the bar, her chardonnay still untouched in front of her. His words came back to him: "I'll back out." Why did he have to say that? He'd been stuck, that's why. He had to sell it to her, get her to come. He'd just gotten carried away in the moment, like always. *Man, now what am I gonna do if she pulls the plug on me?*

Jennifer looked over at him.

So beautiful.

She smiled as if she'd heard his last thought, but the smile was brittle, tense. He reached out and stroked her cheek with the back of his hand. "Let's just relax and have a good time, okay?" he said.

She nodded.

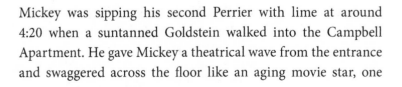

Mickey was sipping his second Perrier with lime at around 4:20 when a suntanned Goldstein walked into the Campbell Apartment. He gave Mickey a theatrical wave from the entrance and swaggered across the floor like an aging movie star, one hand in his pants pocket, his gaze shooting around to see if he recognized anyone, or anyone him. It was the first time Mickey had seen him in over three years. He was still wearing double-breasted suits, this one a bold chalk stripe that hugged him as if it loved him unconditionally. His hair, still only touched by gray at the temples, was slicked straight back. His red tie and pocket square matched.

"Mickey, please don't get up," he said, shaking hands when he reached the table. "Great to see you. You're looking well, old man."

Goldstein looked younger than his 48 years, and younger than the last time Mickey had seen him, because he'd obviously had work done on his face. The puffiness beneath his eyes was gone, the lines at the corners of his mouth had been softened and his jowls were less pronounced. Mickey'd heard that women found Goldstein strikingly handsome, and in that moment he felt a tug in his chest as he realized that Rachel probably did, too.

Goldstein pulled a chair close to Mickey, sat down and said in a loud whisper, "I must say that I think it's unusually civilized that we two can have a social drink and engage in a business deal, given what might ordinarily be an uncomfortable situation. You know, Rachel being your ex and my to-be."

Mickey smiled. "We're adults." He only had to endure another five minutes of that before he saw Jennifer and Paul at the entrance and said, "Here they are now."

They could have been royalty the way they commanded the room as they crossed the floor, a number of heads turning to watch them, Jennifer in a little black dress that highlighted her curves and an opera length strand of pearls, a black clutch in her hand. Paul wore a dark blue European-cut suit with a subtle tie against a white shirt. Both of their faces flashed into broad smiles when they saw Mickey.

Mickey would have stood as they approached anyhow, but given the statement they made, felt compelled to. He checked Jennifer's face for any signs of anger or tension. *Nothing.*

Mickey made introductions when they arrived. Once they were seated, Paul said to Goldstein, "Thanks for agreeing to meet so unfashionably early. I don't know if Mickey told you, but Jennifer and I have opera tickets tonight."

"Oh," Goldstein said. He looked at his watch. "I know how hectic it can be rushing to dinner, then the stress of trying to find a cab to get up to Lincoln Center in time."

Paul said, "A few years ago I discovered the Grand Tier Restaurant right in Lincoln Center. They seat us at 6:30, we have a leisurely dinner, and then just walk across the balcony into the opera house."

Jennifer placed her hand on Paul's arm and said, "At the first intermission we can even go back to the same table for dessert and coffee. It's Paul's secret weapon."

Paul turned to her and they smiled at each other like new lovers.

The waiter came over. Paul said, "I think I'd like to have some wine instead of a cocktail. Anyone else interested?" The waiter handed him the reserve wine list, an inch-thick folio. Paul looked up at Mickey and said, "This place was a good choice. This is a helluva wine list."

Mickey nodded and smiled. Paul was doing great. And not overdoing it, at least so far.

Paul pored over the wine list, flipping back and forth, occasionally pursing his lips. While he looked at it, Goldstein said to Jennifer, "What opera are you seeing tonight?"

"*Carmen.*"

Goldstein said, "Oh, I love *Carmen*. I think it's Bizet's most beautiful music."

Jennifer leaned forward, her face eager, and said, "I agree. I'm a little embarrassed to say I've never actually *seen* it performed. Even though I've been skating to that music since I was a child."

Goldstein raised his eyebrows, interested. "You're a skater?"

"Oh, not for years. I was raised in Michigan—frozen lakes and all that—so skating was obligatory as a child."

"Were you any good?"

"When I was young. I gave it up in junior high when I started banging up my knees and hips from falling."

Mickey could hardly believe it. Jennifer was smiling, easy-going, engaged. Like she had been when talking to Rachel at Hector's Halloween party. Not at all the stone-faced presence she'd been when he was first introduced to her. He didn't know what Paul had said to her, but obviously she was playing along like she was part of the act.

Goldstein said to Jennifer, "And what do you do now?"

"I model women's lingerie."

Mickey saw Goldstein's eyes twitch. Mickey smiled.

Paul looked up from the wine list and said, "Walter, are you a wine drinker?"

"Absolutely."

"You mind if I order something I think we'll all like?"

"I'm in your capable hands," Goldstein said, beaming.

Yuck, Mickey thought.

Paul ordered a 1990 Echezeaux from Mongeard-Mugneret.

Goldstein said to Paul, "Are you a burgundy man?"

Paul said, "Absolutely. I started out loving those huge zinfandels, then migrated to syrah, then to giant California cabernets, eventually appreciating the subtlety of well-aged Bordeaux, finally to burgundy. I think that's where I'll stay."

Goldstein said, "Sounds like a good place to reside. I prefer well-aged Bordeaux, frankly, although I have my favorite burgundy producers. Who are yours?"

"I'm particularly fond of Dujac, Mongeard-Mugneret and Bourée."

"Pierre Bourée," Goldstein said, showing genuine interest.

"Yes, a little-known producer from Gevrey-Chambertin. To my knowledge there's still only one shop in New York that imports it. A small operation on Park Avenue South—"

"Why of course, Quality House!"

"Gary Fraidin. I buy from him all the time."

"As do I," Goldstein said. "And from his father, too, before Gary took over the shop."

"My dad knew his dad," Paul said. "So you know Bourée's wines?"

"He's my favorite burgundy producer. I'm the proprietor of Galerie de Bourée in Soho, named as a tip of the hat to him."

Double yuck, Mickey thought.

The wine arrived. Paul sniffed, swirled, tasted and nodded his approval. The waiter poured.

"What do you think of it?" Goldstein asked Paul.

"I love it. I could go on about hints of raspberry and strawberries in the nose, a good backbone of ripe berries on the palate, the long finish. But I really find I'm happy to just say I do or don't like it. If somebody asks me why, I can tell them with all that analytical stuff, but I find that it takes the enjoyment out of it for me. I'd rather just be left alone to relax and appreciate a glass of wine without saying why."

"Sensible," Goldstein said. He thought for a moment, then said, "Paul, I understand you're in the financial business."

"Yes and no. I guess you could call me an investor. But others manage most of my money today."

"Stocks? Bonds?"

"Mostly hedge funds, some real estate, and a few managed portfolios of individual stocks and bonds. And I do a fair amount of my own investing in art."

Goldstein arched his eyebrows. "Art?" he said, as if he was pleasantly surprised. Mickey thought it was funny, seeing Goldstein stick to the rules for once.

Mickey said, "Walter, I think you and Paul share an interest in art. Why don't you tell him about your business?"

Goldstein elevated his chin and protruded his lower lip. "I've been a dealer all my life, starting on the Continent with a gallery in Paris, and then in London, more recently moving the center of my enterprise to New York. As I said, I currently own a gallery in Soho."

"Where are you from?" Paul asked.

"Originally, Switzerland, but I've lived and worked all over the Continent."

"What kind of art?" Paul asked.

"You might say I've had very eclectic interests throughout my career. In Paris in the '80s I had a gallery devoted to pre-impressionism, impressionism, and postimpressionism, although one's stock in trade is generally contemporary artists of the day, since classic, older pieces rarely become available. But I've made it my business over the years to stay involved whenever major pieces are offered. After that, in the '90s in London, I did a lively trade in Lichtenstein and Warhol."

Paul said, "I went after a Lichtenstein at auction recently."

"Which one?"

"*Ohhh…Alright…*"

Goldstein made his eyes go wide.

Paul said, "Yeah, the price got a little crazy."

"Over $40 million at Christie's as I recall."

"To be exact, $42.6 million."

Goldstein said, "Do you buy mostly privately, through galleries, or at auction?"

Jennifer laughed. "Paul hates auctions."

Paul said, "Chandelier bids, guarantees. I never feel like I'm getting a fair shake."

Mickey felt a flash of surprise, wondering what Paul was talking about. He said, "Chandelier bids?"

Paul said, "They're phony bids the auctioneer simply pretends to see in the house in order to get the process rolling. He's allowed to do it up to the reserve price below which the seller won't sell the artwork."

Jennifer said, "The term comes from the fact that sometimes the auctioneer is literally looking at the chandelier when he announces the bid."

Goldstein said, "The practice is part of the reason most of my clients prefer to deal discreetly through a reputable gallery."

Paul said, "What I hate even worse is that auction houses use guarantees, too. They're arrangements where a third-party bidder agrees to pay a set price for the artwork—guarantees it—to set a solid floor for the bidding, and then gets a cut from the seller of any price that exceeds his guarantee price."

Jennifer said, "The guarantor is even allowed to bid in the auction to drive up the price, and his cut of the excess can range from 30% to 50%."

Goldstein said with a dour face, "Sordid practices."

Paul said, "And yet all perfectly legal in New York."

Goldstein said to Paul, "So you're a fan of Lichtenstein?"

"Yes. More his early 'comic book' stuff from the '60s than his later 'modern painting series,' 'brushstroke series,' or the 'mirrors series.' But one later piece I particularly love is his derivative *Bedroom in Arles* based on van Gogh's painting. I spent hours just staring at it."

"You saw it when it was on loan to the National Gallery?"

"No, my father knew Robert and Jane Meyerhoff, the owners. They let me see it up at their Fitzhugh Farm outside Washington DC."

Goldstein pursed his lips, looking impressed.

They went on like that for another half hour, Paul ordering another bottle of wine, this one a 1986 Lafite Rothschild in deference to Goldstein's preference for aged Bordeaux, with Goldstein going on about "Having an active clientele interested in Warhol, Jasper Johns and Rauschenberg in the '90s when I was established in London," and so on, ad nauseam.

Then Paul and Goldstein got into quite a discussion about Robert Rauschenberg's influence on Jasper Johns, then in turn Johns' influence on Warhol and Lichtenstein. Jennifer chimed in from time to time as well. Mickey found himself smiling as he listened. He had no idea where this was coming from, but if he didn't know better he'd have sworn that Paul actually knew what he was talking about. He loved it. He kept watching Goldstein, who seemed to be buying it all.

After Goldstein spent fifteen minutes talking about his "21st-century enterprise in the Galerie de Bourée in Soho," Mickey finally stood up to use the men's room, motioning with his eyes for Paul to join him.

Halfway across the floor, Mickey said to Paul, "You did great, absolutely great, but did you have to go on about your father knowing that wine shop fellow's father?"

"I was going with the flow. I just got a little carried away."

"It was risky. What if he goes in there and talks to this Gary, the owner, and says he met you?"

"Man, you don't give me much credit, you know that?" Paul said.

Mickey looked over at him, startled.

Paul said, "I *know* Gary at that wine shop. Back in the day when I had the money I really did buy wines from him. I'm no wine maven, man, but I didn't learn everything from you to prepare for this deal. And I wasn't bullshitting about starting out with zinfandels and winding up where I am enjoying burgundies, including Bourée's."

"Sorry," Mickey said. "So you and Jennifer really are going to the opera tonight?"

"You gotta be outta your mind. She can't stand that stuff."

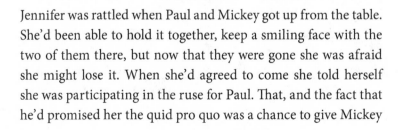

Jennifer was rattled when Paul and Mickey got up from the table. She'd been able to hold it together, keep a smiling face with the two of them there, but now that they were gone she was afraid she might lose it. When she'd agreed to come she told herself she was participating in the ruse for Paul. That, and the fact that he'd promised her the quid pro quo was a chance to give Mickey a piece of her mind about involving Paul in this nonsense, and that he'd given her the okay to ask him to drop out of it.

Now she wished she'd just refused to come at all. The icing on it was being stranded with this smarmy guy who went on and on and on about himself, calling Mickey "old man," patronizing Paul and leering at her. And she hadn't smelled so much cologne since a seventh-grade dance. She couldn't understand what a true lady like Rachel saw in the creep, wished he'd crawl back under his rock.

The moment Mickey and Paul were out of earshot, Goldstein leaned a little closer to her. He went on for a while longer about his art business. Her mind drifted, still holding it together, smiling, nodding.

At one point he said to her, "I'm impressed with your knowledge of art."

Jennifer said, "I picked up all of it through Paul."

Then he moved in his chair so his forearm was touching hers. His cologne was overpowering now. He lowered his voice and said, "Yes, I can see your young man, Paul, is a collector of fine things." He placed his hand on her forearm. "*Including* works of art."

She moved her arm away. "'Things?' Are you intentionally trying to insult me?"

"To the contrary. That's the last thing I'd ever do. I think you're the most beautiful young lady I've ever had the pleasure to lay eyes on. At least in person, not in the cinema."

Oh, please. "So now you're going to offer to put me in the movies?"

Goldstein leaned back again, as if preparing to take a different tack. "May I ask how long you and Paul have been an item?"

An item? "We've been dating for about a year." Jennifer could now feel her muscles tensing.

"And Mickey? How long have you known him?"

"I met him through Paul, but he and Paul have known each other for quite a few years. Through some financial business. I don't really understand the nature of it, but it was when Mickey was still on Wall Street."

Goldstein cocked his head and drooped his eyes like he was sad. "Yes, when he was on Wall Street. That's a chapter that ended badly, poor man."

Jennifer sipped her wine, put it down and studied the glass, feeling Goldstein's gaze on her, but refusing to look back at him.

"I'm only asking about Mickey because I wonder if you're aware of the extent of Mickey's crimes, and the degree to which he's now an outcast from any reputable business endeavor."

Jennifer still didn't meet his gaze.

"I only mention it because it has implications on the character of those who would associate with one as disreputable as Mickey."

Jennifer glanced toward the other end of the room, thinking it was time for Paul and Mickey to return, wanting this to be over.

Goldstein said, "My dear, forgive me if I'm making you tense or uncomfortable, but I'm simply fascinated by you. I'd love to get to know you better, perhaps some time when your young man is out of town on one of his many travels. I'd enjoy showing you the more sophisticated side of New York. You might find it quite intoxicating."

Jennifer still refused to look at him.

He didn't get the hint. He said, "Maybe even get used to being maintained in a certain style by a man who's seen much more of the world. You might find that even more intoxicating."

With that Jennifer turned her head to look him in the eye. "Not likely," she said, and then added through taut lips, "ever, old man."

It was one of those men's rooms with an attendant. Mickey supposed that was part of the Campbell Apartment's image, even the bathrooms from another era. Mickey didn't feel comfortable talking in front of the man, so he stood by the sinks, waiting for Paul while he used the urinal. Paul finished and walked over.

He said, "You don't have to go?"

Mickey shook his head. "I just wanted a minute alone."

As they left the men's room, Mickey decided he didn't need to say anything to Paul after all. His gaze locked on Jennifer. Her body language said it all: she was seated with her back pressed against the chair and her palms on the edge of the table as if she were pushing herself away from Goldstein. Even from across the room, Mickey could see her face was tense, her jaw set. He smiled. *Mission accomplished.* He said, "We should wrap this up."

"Yeah," Paul said. "Paul the art maven needs to get Jennifer up to that opera she's been dying to see."

Paul watched Jennifer's face as Mickey herded them into a cab on Vanderbilt Avenue outside Grand Central. He wasn't sure whether she was pissed at him, Mickey, or the overall situation. She sat in silence between Mickey and him for the whole ride over to the Chelsea, where Mickey had insisted they go to have their talk.

When they got upstairs to their room, Jennifer glanced around, taking in the place, then threw off her wrap and sat down on the sofa with her arms and legs crossed. "Let's get this all out on the table," she said. She looked up at Mickey, who was standing by the refrigerator and opening a bottle of Perrier, and said, "You set that up!"

Mickey said to her, "Set up what?"

Paul was standing next to Jennifer, thinking, *Yeah, what?*, looking back and forth at each of them.

Jennifer said to Mickey, "You knew what he was going to do."

Mickey said to her, "How could I have known anything that he was going to do?"

Paul thinking, *What the hell is going on?* Still looking back and forth at each of them, Paul said, "What did he do?"

Jennifer said to Mickey, "You knew he would!"

Paul said, "Knew he'd what?"

Mickey said to Jennifer, "I know what kind of man he is, but how on earth could I predict what he'd do?"

Jennifer said to Mickey, "He's a slimeball."

Paul still thinking, *What the hell is going on?* He looked at Mickey with the bottle of Perrier in his hand, then at Jennifer sitting with her arms and legs crossed even tighter now, her jaw rigid, glaring at Mickey.

Mickey said, "He's worse than a slimeball."

Paul raised his voice. "Can anybody hear me? What the hell did he do?"

Jennifer finally looked at Paul and said, "Goldstein made a pass at me!"

Paul said, "Goldstein? That old fart? Man, the guy must be at least 50." He turned and saw Mickey widen his eyes. "Sorry, Mickey." But Paul couldn't restrain a belly laugh. "That's hilarious. I wish I'd seen it."

Jennifer threw him a look that gave him a chill, then stared off at the wall.

Paul decided this was bullshit. If that's all this was about, Goldstein hitting on Jennifer, she'd get over it. They had more important things to discuss.

Paul walked over and sat down across from Jennifer in one of the cushioned chairs. Mickey sat down in the other one, the three of them now faced off against one another in a triangle. Paul said, "I thought we came here to talk about this deal."

Mickey looked over at Paul and smiled. "Yes, I think that's why we're here," Mickey said. "Jennifer, how about I tell you what this is all about, since I gather you're upset because you think I'm going to land your man in jail again."

Jennifer let out a sigh, and said, "Yes, that's a story I'd love to hear."

Mickey lowered his voice, talking almost inaudibly, the way he did when he was most effective. Paul always wondered if he did it on purpose so people would have to lean forward and strain to hear him, give him their full attention. Mickey said, "So now you've had a taste of Goldstein. You've spent some time with me, too. And you've met Rachel. So here's the situation." He paused, his eyes blinking like they did when he was thinking. "It's all about Goldstein." He looked over at Paul like he was apologetic. "I only brought in these other well-heeled bidders to get Goldstein to pay more."

Paul looked at Jennifer, who had now relaxed on the sofa, one arm over the side, her legs extended, listening, her brow wrinkled.

Mickey said, "I knew Goldstein before I went to jail. Yes, he's actually an art dealer. But I did my due diligence on him and I could never find out enough about him to know where he really came from. I never found those galleries in Paris or London he talked about today. I did find him in Switzerland, but only at some boarding school when he was in his teens. But after that, very little."

"What's your point?" Jennifer said.

"The point is that I got the idea for this whole deal—Paul being some highly cultured, wealthy art collector who buys and sells paintings for millions, even stolen ones—from my impressions of Goldstein. I think the man's a complete fraud."

Mickey leaned forward in his chair, put his elbows on his knees, his hands clasped in front of him, looking straight at Jennifer.

"So put yourself in my situation. I get indicted, convicted, stripped of my securities licenses and sent to jail. While that's all happening, Rachel, my wife of over 20 years, divorces me, takes half my assets and the rest of them get vaporized in legal fees and fines."

Jennifer's and Mickey's gazes were locked on each other's.

"Then, when I'm ready to get out of jail, I find out that not only is Goldstein living in my old apartment with my ex-wife, but that he's engaged to her, and half of all my former assets that she now owns have been disappeared into some void by Goldstein, presumably into artwork in his business."

"So this is about you wanting your money back," Jennifer said.

"This is about me wanting my wife back."

"Really?" Jennifer said.

"Yes, although I wouldn't mind getting my money back, too. But more important than that, I can't stand the idea of Goldstein having it, even if I can't get Rachel back."

Jennifer nodded as if she understood.

Paul was smiling, watching the two of them. He could see where Mickey was leading Jennifer. He only wished he could talk to her this way. Him, the one who was supposed to be the talker.

Mickey said, "So here's the whole deal. We snooker Goldstein into paying as much as we can for the painting, and then I wait and see what happens with Rachel and him before I make my move on Rachel again. Because I think I need some time for things to heal with her, having blown it at Hector's Halloween party—"

"You didn't blow it at Hector's Halloween party," Jennifer said. "You were on the right track, trust me. Make your move once you've handled Goldstein."

"I hope you're right. But either way I need to get Rachel free of him. And I'm going to wreck the bastard while I do it."

Jennifer laughed at that, and Paul saw that she couldn't get rid of the smile it left her with. Finally she said, "That has a certain appeal, I have to admit. Alright, if Goldstein's the only target, I'm in."

Mickey said, "That's great, but I don't need you to be in. I just need you to stand aside and let us work."

"Yes, you do need me. You think that riff at cocktails about Roy Lichtenstein and Andy Warhol's antecedents in Robert Rauschenberg via Jasper Johns, as evidenced in the commonality of their early works like Lichtenstein's *Drowning Girl* and Warhol's *Turquoise Marilyn*, then their artistic divergence as they both matured, blah blah blah, or Jackson Pollock's anguish showing in the dark nihilism of his last abstract expressionist paintings was Mr. Paul Reece talking?"

Mickey laughed. "Go on," he said.

"Come on, guys. Flashcards? Janson's *History of Art* as your only resource? That's not going to get it done. I assume Paul told you I've got my master's in art history. If I hadn't coached him for a full day before meeting Goldstein, you guys would've been fried by the time the first bottle of wine was gone. You need me. I'm in."

Well I'll be, Mickey thought. He'd been shocked out of his shorts twice in two days, first by Goldstein offering to preempt, now by Jennifer. He wondered if she wanted her own cut, if she'd take half of Paul's, or maybe was only doing it because she couldn't stand Goldstein. He'd worry about that later. He had to admit, Paul had been spectacular at cocktails, and he now realized it was largely due to Jennifer.

Jennifer said, "So how does this preemptive thing work for Goldstein to buy the painting?"

Mickey said, "I'm not sure it works at all."

Paul spun to Mickey. "Yeah. We've got all these big fish on the line, Buffett, Gates, Murdoch. You're not really serious about walking away from those guys if one of them might pay more than Goldstein, are you? It doesn't make sense to me, and it doesn't seem like you, Mickey, even considering Rachel."

Jennifer's eyes shot daggers at Paul. Mickey spoke up before she could unleash. "As I said earlier, we've only got them in the hunt to push Goldstein higher. Anytime you sell something, the best way to keep the buyer honest is for him to know he's got competition, right down to the last second. In mergers and acquisitions when you're selling a company, the ideal situation is to have two bidders in separate conference rooms at your law firm negotiating the contract at the same time, and make sure they both know it. Usually the second buyer is just a stalking horse to keep the first buyer honest. But sometimes you get pleasantly surprised by your stalking horse. At any event, the first bidder isn't going to reach to pay top dollar unless he knows he's likely to lose if he doesn't."

Jennifer said, "That doesn't sound at all to me the way Paul described having Goldstein preempt. He said you'd shut down all the other buyers and do the deal with Goldstein one-on-one. Why can't we do that and take the $40 million he's desperate to pay us?"

Us, Mickey thought. This Jennifer was a piece of work, moving right in.

Mickey said, "Because we're talking about Goldstein. I think you get the picture of the kind of person we're dealing with now. We've already called all our buyers, and even started setting up the first-round bid. All the experts are talking to each other and this process leaks like crazy. So if we actually shut down the process or even put it on hold to try and do a deal with Goldstein, my guess is he'll find out in a heartbeat."

Jennifer was nodding her head as if she understood.

"The second he finds that out, his $40 million goes to 30, maybe even $20 million. At that point if we tell Goldstein to take a hike and restart our process, who knows? We may have lost some bidders because we've jerked them around. Or they may feel like we're offering them distressed merchandise because we put them on hold and then somehow couldn't do a deal with whoever our lead party was. And we've come limping back to them with no negotiating leverage."

Paul said, "So what do we do, man?"

"I haven't thought it through yet, but I think we should tell Goldstein no deal on preempting. Even though he's threatened that his number will drop, or he'll even withdraw entirely if we revert to an auction process." Mickey looked up at the ceiling, thinking. "But we tell him we're going back to a single-stage bid process—meet-and-greets and viewings with buyers and their experts—with a handful of parties we feel are most capable and get it over with quickly, asking for final bids and closing a deal within a week."

Paul said, "You think Goldstein will stick?"

"He can taste it now. If he sees it's only a week away, yes, I think he'll stick."

Mickey hoped he wasn't just believing his own bullshit.

Goldstein didn't at all like what Mickey had to tell him the next morning: that they were declining Goldstein's preemptive offer and proceeding with the auction, albeit on an accelerated time-table and with a limited, exclusive handful of bidders. Mickey had called all of them already, they had agreed to the process and were awaiting instructions on setting up viewings. Goldstein groused about the absurdity of trying to extract more than the $40 million he'd offered, going on about it for another five min-utes. When Mickey asked him if he was in or out, Goldstein tried not to answer, said he'd get back to him once he'd cooled off. He said he considered Mickey's reversal a complete betrayal, an ungentlemanly act of an avaricious neophyte in the art world.

Mickey made sure he didn't laugh into the phone, then pressed
Goldstein again, who finally admitted that he was still in. "But
price, well, we'll just have to see about that, old man."

CHAPTER 5

Late that afternoon Mickey got out of a cab just after Lafayette Street became Federal Plaza, and then walked across Foley Square to the U.S. Attorney's Office at 1 St. Andrew's Plaza. He'd been here often enough when he was indicted and working on his plea bargain, and being here again gave Mickey the creepiest feeling he'd had since walking into Yankton over three years ago. Charlie Holden, the Assistant U.S. Attorney in New York, had summoned Mickey here today, Holden not even making the call himself, but delegating it to his assistant. Mickey was aware that Rachel had identified Moravian White, Dontelle White's brother, from a mug shot shortly after White had pistol-whipped her, and that Holden's men and the NYPD hadn't been able to find White ever since. He hoped this meeting had something to do with White.

But as he climbed the granite steps to the doorway into the building, framed by massive Corinthian columns, he had an ominous feeling because he didn't think it did.

When he got upstairs, Holden kept Mickey waiting for 20 minutes before his assistant waved Mickey into his office. Holden was talking on the phone. He looked a little paunchier, a little grayer, but still as angry and hostile as ever. Holden looked at Mickey over the top of his glasses and pointed to a chair in front of his desk. He finished his phone call, put the phone down and sat back. He said, "I can't believe what I've been hearing."

Mickey decided to play dumb. "They still can't find Moravian White?"

"In the interest of doing my job I guess we should dispense with that before I tell you why I called you over here." He paused, staring into Mickey's eyes.

Is this supposed to scare me?

Holden said, "We haven't been able to locate Moravian White. He hasn't been near his apartment since our men first showed up there. Not at work, either. At work they insist he's on vacation but we know that's bullshit."

Mickey waited for Holden to go on.

"We've pulled the team from your friend's apartment but we still have two of our people watching your ex-wife's apartment. No sightings. We're staying on it." Now he leaned forward and put his elbows on his desk. "But that's not why I called you in here."

Surprise.

"I'm getting calls telling me that you're passing yourself off as an art dealer and trying to sell some painting. Worse than that, I hear it's a famous stolen masterpiece. Even worse than that, you've got major hitters involved, and we're talking about tens of millions of dollars."

Mickey felt his pulse shoot up, but he forced himself to keep his demeanor calm, taking it in, thinking, waiting.

"No response?" Holden leaned farther forward over his desk.

Mickey had to admit, Holden had perfected the menacing stare. But somehow it didn't work as well sitting in his office as it did when you were freezing in an interrogation room they kept at 60 degrees. But that wasn't the issue. The man wasn't clairvoyant, but his information was dead-on accurate. One of the buyers must have tipped off Holden. Trying to queer the process in order to get an unfair advantage, come back and try to negotiate a deal without going through the bidding. *Or is one of the experts Holden's stooge?*

"I don't know what you're talking about," Mickey said.

Holden just continued to stare him down, then said, "And I understand you're living here in town with some knucklehead you met at Yankton. Is he part of this thing, too?"

"I do have a friend here in New York that I met at Yankton, although I wouldn't call him a knucklehead."

Holden reached over to the side of his desk and opened a folder. He pulled his glasses down, peered over them. "Paul Reece. Our office prosecuted him in the last year. Belcher Securities, a pump and dump operation that he was in the center of. Sentenced to Yankton."

"Yes, that would be my friend Paul. But, as I said, he's no knucklehead."

Holden snapped the folder shut and looked back at Mickey, then threw an arm out to point a finger at his nose. "I'm not screwing around here. I could probably have you sent back even on suspicion of something like this. I'm putting you on notice. You pull any hijinks in my jurisdiction and you're going away again. And if you think South Dakota was cold, wait till you see where I'll send you this time."

Mickey said, "How about we talk again about this Moravian White?"

"Don't get cute. You shut down your little art scam, now. Or you and your knucklehead friend will freeze your asses off this winter."

Moravian White, standing in his hoodie outside Bergdorf Goodman, made the *gong!* sound of a pinball machine when he saw the Steinberg woman walking out the door onto 58th Street. *My lucky day.* An hour ago he'd watched from across the street on Park Avenue as she stepped out of her apartment building and into a cab that headed across town. The traffic was light so the cab went fast and he couldn't keep up on foot without running, so he guessed Bergdorf Goodman today. Forty-five minutes waiting across the street, milling around in front of the Plaza Hotel, over by the Apple Store in front of the GM Building, and now here she was. He started across 58th Street toward her.

She stopped at the curb, bags in her hands, looking around, must be for a cab. When she started walking over to a line of cabs in front of the Plaza Hotel, he picked up his pace and fell in behind her. He had the Glock in the right pocket of his hoodie. When he got behind her he grabbed her arm with his left hand and poked the Glock into her back.

"Don't say nothing and you won't get hurt. If you yell out you're dead."

She turned with her mouth open and eyes wide.

"Yeah, it's me again. You gonna behave?"

The woman nodded her head.

"Good, let's take a walk. Up Fifth Avenue alongside the park makes a nice stroll this time of day, don't you think?"

They crossed over to Fifth Avenue and started uptown.

"Where is he?"

The woman didn't answer.

"Don't hold out on me, 'cause I know you know where he is now."

"You promise to leave me alone if I tell you?" the woman said, her voice all trembling.

There's a nice lady. "That's right."

"He's at the Chelsea Hotel on 23rd Street, room 3B."

"Okay, you keep walking and don't turn around, 'cause I'm right behind you. You turn around and I'll shoot."

Moravian thought to give her a little poke in the ribs with the Glock before he walked away, but saw no sense in it, so he just turned around and headed down Fifth Avenue, running his thumb up and down the pistol grip of the Glock, smiling.

Mickey turned his cell phone back on and called Paul as soon as he left 1 St. Andrew's Plaza.

"Where are you?" he asked Paul.

"At the Chelsea. Everything okay?"

"No. Is Jennifer with you?"

"Yeah. What's wrong?"

"Get Jennifer out of there, put the painting in a suitcase or a shopping bag, anything, and have her take it up to her apartment."

"What happened?"

"Just do it. Holden knows everything. Somebody tipped him off. Get Jennifer and the painting out of there and I'll see you as soon as I can get there. Then we'll head up to Jennifer's to figure out what we do."

"Does Holden know where we're staying?"

"He knows we're staying together, so he has to. He must have talked to our parole officers. So have Jennifer go alone, because

Holden's people probably won't recognize her if they're watching, but they'll know you."

Mickey hailed a cab to head back to the Chelsea, still trying to figure it out.

Mickey's cell phone rang just as he got out of the cab in front of the Chelsea.

"Mickey!" Rachel said, sounding frantic. Mickey could hear sounds of traffic in the background, horns honking. "Are you okay?"

"Yes, why?"

"Are you at the Chelsea?" Her voice was shaking.

"Just getting here." He stood out on the sidewalk, listening to her labored breathing into the phone. Now his own heart started pumping.

"You have to get out of there. That man, that Caribbean man, whatever his name is, he found me."

"Are you alright?"

"Yes, but he held a gun to me again. Right out on the street. I—I'm sorry, Mickey, but I was so frightened I told him you're staying at the Chelsea. You have to get out of there."

"How long ago?"

"I'm not sure, maybe 15 minutes ago. Maybe more. He grabbed me outside Bergdorf's and we walked up Fifth Avenue. He told me if I turned around he'd shoot me. When I finally got up the nerve to look behind me he was gone. I've been trying to call you but it's been going to voicemail."

"Call the police. Then go someplace safe, a friend's, but not back to the apartment until the police come to you wherever you go. You hear me?"

"Yes, but you get out of there. Call me later."

Mickey hung up and ran into the lobby of the Chelsea. Rachel hadn't been certain how much time had passed, so he'd just run upstairs, get Paul and get out of there.

He should've been here by now, Paul thought, checking his watch again as he paced around their room in the Chelsea, waiting for Mickey. Jennifer had left 10 minutes earlier with the painting, so she and it were safe, but this whole thing was twisting in his mind. He couldn't believe somebody would actually go so far as to call the Feds about the painting just to get an edge in the process, but he couldn't think of any other reason somebody would do it.

Unless somebody who really hated Mickey got word of the deal and wanted to sabotage him. He'd get a better handle on it when Mickey arrived. Then the two of them could talk it through.

He heard the key in the lock. *Finally.* Mickey came through the door, his face grim, almost no color in it. He slammed the door behind him and started across the room.

"We need to get out of here, now," Mickey said.

"What the hell's going on?"

"Moravian White found Rachel again. He held a gun on her and she told him we're—I'm staying here. He's coming." Mickey's eyes were glazed.

Paul's cop training and instincts clicked in. He grabbed Mickey by the shoulders and spun him around, ushered him toward the door. He put command in his voice as he said, "Let me handle this."

Paul got Mickey downstairs as fast as he could, then in the lobby grabbed him by the coat sleeve and stopped him beside the door.

"You wait here. I'll check outside first." He walked over to reception and bummed a cigarette from Xavier behind the desk, then went outside and lit the cigarette by the front door, stood around like he'd just stepped outside for a smoke.

He tried not to be too obvious about looking around the neighborhood. He remembered Mickey saying Rachel described the man as dark, Caribbean black. This was New York, so that description wasn't much help, and it was about 5:00 in the afternoon, the streets already crowded with people leaving from work or going home after shopping. He didn't see anybody hanging around as if they were waiting or watching. He dropped the cigarette, snuffed it out and walked back inside.

He said to Mickey, "Okay, get outside, into a cab and up to Jennifer's. I'll stay behind like I don't know you and watch. I'll meet you up there."

Mickey's face had gotten some color back in it, but his eyes were still glassy. He nodded to Paul as he listened, clearly scared out of his wits, Paul again trying to keep the authority in his voice to calm him down.

Paul walked outside first, stepped over to the curb like he was looking for a cab, still observing through trained eyes, looking for sudden movements, anything. Mickey came out and stepped to the curb about 10 feet away from Paul.

That's when Paul saw the man burst through the door of a clothing store across the street. Dark-skinned black, wearing a hoodie with his hands in his pockets. *White!* He headed straight through between two parked cars and out into the street. He had to stop to let a sanitation truck lumber past.

"Run!" Paul yelled while White was screened behind the truck. He saw Mickey break into a run toward Eighth Avenue. Paul stepped between two parked cars and out into the street, on a line to intercept the guy, trying to slow the pace of his walk as if he was just crossing the street. He could feel his fingers trembling from adrenaline, hear his pulse pounding in his ears.

As soon as the truck passed, White was out in the middle of the street, walking fast, looking directly where Mickey had been before he started running. White looked to his right and saw Mickey, then started to run after him. Paul was only a few feet from him so he took a long stride and stuck his foot out, tripped the guy. His heart was thundering as he said, "Oh, sorry, man."

White glared back at him as he got up and started running after Mickey.

"Hey! Stop that man! He's got a gun!" Paul yelled and ran for the other side of the street.

White turned and held out a gun—it looked like a semi-automatic—and hollered, "Bet your ass!" and pointed it at Paul.

Paul dived between two cars at the curb, expecting to feel the bullet, hear the shot, but nothing. He crawled around the side of the car and stuck his head up, saw White running after Mickey down 23rd Street, Mickey with a lead of about 25 yards.

Paul started running down the sidewalk in the same direction. "Call the police!" he yelled. "Gun! That man has a gun!"

Son of a bitch! The crazy man actually pulled up, held out the gun toward Mickey and popped off a round right there in a street full of people. Then another two shots. He heard people scream and saw them dive to the sidewalk. Mickey started zigzagging, still making a break toward Eighth Avenue. White started running again when he saw Mickey getting away. White was fast, like he'd played wide receiver, sprinting down the side of the street, Mickey dodging pedestrians on the sidewalk, doing pretty good for a pudgy guy in his 50s but White was catching up. When Mickey was about 50 yards from the corner of Eighth Avenue, the nutcase slowed down and fired two more wild rounds, holding the gun out sideways like the morons in the movies did. At that point Paul came to a big gap between parked cars and slanted into the street, picking up ground on White. "Gun!" Paul yelled again. "He's got a gun!" but White didn't turn or react, just kept on, again gaining ground on Mickey. Paul's lungs were starting to burn as he ran flat out, thinking how he'd distract White if he caught up to him, draw him off Mickey without presenting himself as a clear target. Paul saw Mickey reach Eighth Avenue and turn north, disappearing around the corner.

"Gun!" Paul yelled again as White turned north onto Eighth Avenue. When Paul rounded the corner onto Eighth Avenue he saw Mickey had crossed to the other side, White angling across the avenue toward him. White got to the middle of the avenue, pulled up and fired again at Mickey, who'd given up on zigzagging and ran straight up the left lane of the avenue.

Paul saw a cop step off the curb a block ahead and unholster his revolver. *Finally.*

"Stop or I'll shoot!" the cop yelled and held his revolver out with both arms in firing position.

No way he takes that shot out here on the street.

Paul kept running as White took a hard right away from the cop, crossed the avenue and ran into 25th Street. The cop took off after him. As Paul passed him he saw Mickey jump into a cab. When he saw that, Paul turned left and ran as fast as he could in the opposite direction down 25th Street. At Ninth Avenue he turned north, then started walking, trying to look normal, like nothing was happening. He hailed the first cab he saw and got in, panting, his hands sweating. It took him 15 blocks to catch his breath.

Some deal, man. Never thought I'd almost get killed trying to sell a painting.

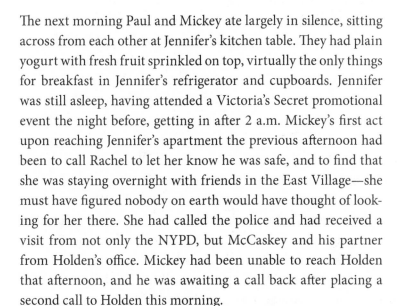

The next morning Paul and Mickey ate largely in silence, sitting across from each other at Jennifer's kitchen table. They had plain yogurt with fresh fruit sprinkled on top, virtually the only things for breakfast in Jennifer's refrigerator and cupboards. Jennifer was still asleep, having attended a Victoria's Secret promotional event the night before, getting in after 2 a.m. Mickey's first act upon reaching Jennifer's apartment the previous afternoon had been to call Rachel to let her know he was safe, and to find that she was staying overnight with friends in the East Village—she must have figured nobody on earth would have thought of looking for her there. She had called the police and had received a visit from not only the NYPD, but McCaskey and his partner from Holden's office. Mickey had been unable to reach Holden that afternoon, and he was awaiting a call back after placing a second call to Holden this morning.

Mickey was now calm and clearheaded, having had the entire night to relive hundreds of times in his head his mad dash on 23rd and up Eighth Avenue. Halfway through the evening he realized he was so shaken by running for his life, actually getting shot at, that he decided to forget about drawing any conclusions or making any decisions until morning.

Mickey looked up at Paul, seeing him through different eyes after the way he'd intervened to stop White the previous afternoon. He said, "You probably did save my life."

Paul looked up and smiled. "You said that about 10 times last night. This is today. Let's move on. Now what?"

Mickey shook off the image of White running after him as he looked back, ready to turn up Eighth Avenue off 23rd Street. He said, "I think this might be enough to distract Holden for a few days, keep him from pressuring us. I figure it gives us breathing space to get a deal done."

Paul's face lit up, first with that boyish grin, then a full-blown smile. "I was hoping you'd say something like that."

Mickey said, "I figure the field is as follows: Buffett, Gates, Murdoch, Geffen, Wynn and Goldstein. And I think I have an idea how we can compress this into only a couple of days. We'll need Jennifer's help, so hopefully she doesn't have shoots for a few days."

"Nothing I'm aware of," Paul said. "But you're pushing it. We'll never get through it in a couple of days."

"We'll stream each of the buyers in serially. We'll even keep moving around from hotel to hotel. That way even if Holden is watching we can minimize our chances of him zeroing in on us."

"Yeah, but he only needs to catch us at one of them."

"I've got some ideas for that, too. I'll start making calls to the buyers after I hear back from Holden. And once Jennifer gets up we can set up our logistics and a timetable."

Paul said, "We still haven't talked about who tipped off Holden."

"I've thought about that, too."

"Whoever it is doesn't need to know Holden. I'm sure the U.S. Attorney's Office has tip hotlines for that kind of thing. It could be any one of the buyers."

Mickey said, "There's only one of these men who's sleazy enough to pull something like that. It has to be Goldstein."

Mickey went back to his yogurt and Paul got up and walked into the bedroom. He came back with a shoe box. He put it on the table, removed the top and pulled out a gun.

Mickey felt a surge of blood to his face, recoiled from the gun. "What's that for?"

"Just in case," Paul said. He pulled a small holster from the box, put his foot up on a chair and strapped the holster to his ankle. "Most cops carry one of these in addition to their service revolvers. A snub-nosed .38 with the serial number filed off. If you ever have to use it you can wipe it clean and drop it in the street. If I'd had it on me yesterday I would've pulled it on that nutcase, White. If he comes again I'll be ready." He stuck the revolver into the holster.

———◆———

Holden returned Mickey's calls about midmorning. Mickey went on the offensive, telling Holden that his sterling efforts to protect Rachel could've gotten her killed, and almost got *him* killed. Holden wanted to know where Mickey was staying. Mickey said he hadn't changed his address from the one he'd reported to his parole officer a few weeks ago: the Chelsea Hotel. Holden said they couldn't find him there. Mickey said Moravian White didn't have any trouble. Holden told him to come downtown to talk about it. Mickey said no thanks, that until Holden demonstrated that he was more focused on keeping Mickey alive than on believing some fantasy about Paul and him doing some crazy art deal, he'd decline the invitation. Mickey's final words were, "Just make sure you protect Rachel. Then maybe in a few days I'll come in and we'll talk."

It was a treat putting Holden back on his heels for once. He needed it to stay that way for at least a few days.

After Jennifer woke up, Paul, she and Mickey spent a few hours going over their strategy and logistics for the next few days. After that, Mickey called all the buyers. Goldstein was his last call.

"I've been eagerly anticipating your call, old man."

"Good," Mickey said. "We're ready to go. Same process as I described to you in our last call. A handful of buyers, compressed time frame. All meetings and viewings to be completed by the end of the day after tomorrow. Single stage auction, one chance to give it your best shot. No callbacks, no negotiations, no rebids. No exceptions. Consideration in Internet gold bitcoin currency only. Final bids due 9 p.m. the day after tomorrow."

Mickey paused, waiting for a response from Goldstein. When there was none, Mickey said, "Any questions?"

"My, that's a very confident tone you're taking. Still a handful of bidders?"

"That's right."

Mickey heard Goldstein exhale and then chuckle. "Alright, I'll play along. When's my viewing?"

"Day after tomorrow, 4 p.m. We'll pick you up by car at 3:30. Where do you want us to get you?"

Goldstein chuckled again. "Why, our apartment, of course, old man."

Mickey hung up, turned to Jennifer and Paul and said, "It must have been Goldstein who called Holden's office. He wouldn't have been so smug otherwise. He thinks he's got us by the short hairs, thinks Holden would have scared us into shutting down the process, leaving Goldstein to cherry-pick us. We'll need to do something else to convince Goldstein we have other buyers in the process."

Jennifer said, "How do we do that?"

"We bring in a new buyer with a really big mouth who'll blab it around so Goldstein can't help but get wind of it."

Paul said, "Where do we scare up somebody like that on short notice?"

"I already called him. We're having dinner with him tonight."

———◆———

Paul wasn't sure if he could feel his blood pumping because he was excited about their upcoming dinner, or because his senses were filled with Jennifer's perfume and the warmth of her body pressed against him in the backseat of a cab.

"I met John Chiusolo about 10 years ago," Mickey said from the other side of the backseat, as the cab inched along 51st Street toward Le Bernardin.

Mickey had reserved Le Bernardin's private dining room in the back. He explained that the private dining room would shield the other patrons from Chiusolo's voice, which was always about 10 decibels above everyone else's, and yet the room was glass-enclosed and visible through the corridor toward the restrooms. As such, anyone walking past would see Chiusolo having an opulent dinner with Mickey and some younger man with a gorgeous woman, a tipoff that Chiusolo and Mickey were working on a big deal. That would hopefully get the word out around town and have it find its way to Goldstein if the magic of Chiusolo's mouth alone wasn't enough to accomplish that.

Mickey continued as the cab stopped yet again in traffic, explaining that Chiusolo started out as a small electrical contractor in Jersey City, then built his business into doing general construction management, from there working his way into projects as a subcontractor with the big builders in the area—Jersey City, Newark, Elizabeth, Kearney—and then struck gold with projects at Hackensack University Medical Center. He'd been brought in as a subcontractor on projects by Angelli Brothers Construction, deeply entrenched with Hackensack Medical for 20 years. After five years of 24/7 service, attention to detail, and schmoozing, Chiusolo elbowed the Angellis aside as the hospital's go-to contractor. That leapfrogged him into the main man in demand for major construction deals in the Angellis' stomping ground.

"When I met him 10 years ago he used to say he was the 'top contractor for the top hospital in New Jersey,' and wanted me to sell his business because he was looking to retire early at 50. We sold it for $1.2 billion to Straight & White in the UK, and after his three-year consulting contract and non-compete were up, Chiusolo was out doing deals again with his old clients, including Hackensack Medical. Today he's got a $500 million construction company and over $1 billion in the bank."

Paul leaned forward to see past Jennifer between them, taking in Mickey's words.

Mickey went on. "About five years ago Chiusolo got bored with powerboats, Jet Skis, snowmobiles, Porsches and Lamborghinis and started collecting art. He recently paid $19 million for a watercolor version of Cézanne's *The Card Players*, $14 million for Picasso's *Le Viol*, both of which people believe he overpaid for. He also tells me confidentially, if you can believe he tells anyone anything confidentially, that he's an active buyer of stolen artwork as well."

"Sounds like he's a serious buyer for my piece," Paul said, already in character.

"Don't get too carried away," Mickey said. "Remember, he's only here as our shill for Goldstein."

Mickey smiled, a broad one.

"You don't look like you mean that," Paul said.

He chuckled. "I'm only smiling because I can't help my nose twitching as I think about Chiusolo, a man who always pays up to get his hands on something he really wants."

"So even if Goldstein offers an outrageous amount for *View of the Sea*, Chiusolo'll pay whatever it takes to trump him?"

"Down, boys," Jennifer said. "Let's stay on plan."

Mickey said, "Chiusolo will probably drive up in a Bentley. He gets a new one every year, always black. He has the horns altered so they're about 25% louder than stock. And he honks a lot, so if you don't see the man, you can't miss hearing him."

"Maybe we should get out and walk," Jennifer said. "I think we've only gone about 20 feet in the last five minutes."

Paul said, "This from a woman in three-inch heels."

Just then the traffic opened up, and they cruised to the entrance to Le Bernardin. They had all gotten out of the cab and reassembled, ready to enter, when a white stretch limo pulled up beside them. The back window rolled down and somebody barked out, "Mickey, how you doin,' bro?" The door opened and Chiusolo stepped out, his raincoat draped around his shoulders like a cape, as if he were William Shatner entering the red carpet in his glory years. A guy stepped out from behind Chiusolo wearing a suit, hunching like a cowed puppy, and said, "You want me to take this, Mr. Chiusolo?"

Chiusolo just hitched back his shoulders and the guy caught his raincoat as it slid off him. The guy folded it over his arm and stood by as if for further instructions.

Chiusolo half turned his head, said, "Thanks, Johnny," and stepped forward. He extended his hand to Mickey and shook. "Mickey," he said, shaking hard. "Great to see you." Paul could see the warmth in Chiusolo's smile.

Mickey introduced Jennifer and Paul. When Chiusolo and Paul shook, Paul noted it was a rough hand, that of a tradesman who'd never given up the urge to swing a hammer.

Mickey smiled and said, "Where's your Bentley?"

"Home. They don't have valet parking here."

"Are you going to the prom in that thing after dinner?"

Chiusolo shot him a look. "They didn't have a black one available."

The captain seated them at a single table in the back private dining room, glass walls on three sides. The room was shielded from the restaurant by its only solid wall, and exposed to the sheen of stainless steel and the beehive of chefs and waitstaff in the kitchen by glass on the opposite wall. A corridor to the restrooms was visible through the glass on one side, a corridor for the waitstaff between the kitchen and the restaurant on the other. The aromas of seafood cooking, mingled with the scents of garlic, herbes de Provence and mirepoix, permeated the room.

After they were seated, Paul stood and insisted Chiusolo move to take the seat facing the kitchen. "I understand you like to cook," Paul said, another tidbit Mickey had told them.

"How'd you know that?"

Paul took the seat facing Chiusolo and flashed a grin. "You may have a bigger reputation than you think."

Paul saw flare-ups from pans in the kitchen reflected on the far wall and in Chiusolo's eyes, heard food sizzling, staccato kitchen commands and the clank of utensils on stainless steel. He looked over at Jennifer, who was smiling, easygoing and relaxed, obviously enjoying the place. When he glanced at Mickey in the seat beside him, he thought he saw a fleeting, pleased smile.

Paul had expected Chiusolo to do some probing into his bona fides, but instead he was all over the place, talking about current construction projects, the addition he was putting on his Jersey Shore house and his daughter's upcoming wedding. They made more small talk through glasses of white burgundy that Paul ordered for the appetizers. Halfway through the entrees, Paul decided it was time to get down to business. He leaned forward and put his forearms on the table, then glanced at Mickey, who smiled and nodded his approval almost imperceptibly. Paul said, "So, John, I asked Mickey to invite you tonight because I understand you've done a few major art deals recently."

"Yeah," Chiusolo said. "I've been collecting for a while now."

Paul said, "A Cézanne and a Picasso in the last 24 months. Impressive."

Chiusolo nodded and smiled back, sipping the red burgundy Paul had chosen for the entrees.

Paul said, "*The Card Players* is a classic. I can't believe you paid only $19 million for it."

Chiusolo shrugged. "It's a watercolor version, after all."

"Still, it looks to me like you stole it."

Chiusolo looked down at his plate, put a forkful of black bass in his mouth, then looked back up, chewing and grinning.

"And I hear you buy pieces that've been, let's say, unavailable for a while." Paul figured he'd take a stab at a little more flattery.

"Have I heard correctly that you bought a Rembrandt that was last seen in Boston, say, over 20 years ago?"

Chiusolo's face went blank, and Paul wondered if he'd screwed up. Three Rembrandts were among the paintings stolen in the Boston Isabella Stewart Gardner Museum heist in 1990. Paul figured Chiusolo would never admit he hadn't bought one of them, because he'd love the idea that they might believe he had. But Chiusolo just looked down at his plate for a long moment.

Man, *had* the guy bought one of the hot pieces?

But then Chiusolo came back up smirking even more broadly. "You never know," he said.

Paul glanced at Mickey, who was doing his best to appear to be the advisor blending into the scenery while his client took the lead, eating his meal, eyes blinking in that lazy way of his. Paul made eye contact again with Chiusolo and held it. "So I gather that means you're used to doing strictly confidential deals, and that you're comfortable owning a piece of art you have to keep under wraps."

"I know the drill."

"Then can I assume from the fact that you accepted Mickey's invitation tonight that we might be able to do a deal together?"

"No doubt about it. The food and company are great, but that's not the reason any of us are here."

Paul nodded and smiled. He decided to defer any further talk about the painting until later. He felt like he'd done his job so far, so he'd wait for Mickey's lead. And he saw how much fun Jennifer was having. She was totally herself, not like the role-playing she'd done at cocktails with Goldstein, even seeming to genuinely like Chiusolo.

They'd finished their entrees, ready for dessert, Chiusolo expounding on how his roofer didn't know how to talk to his clients, and how his man from New York, Tony Lorenzo, was screwing up his electrical contract on the new switching station for the MTA, when Paul got up to go to the restroom.

"I'll go, too," Mickey said.

In the corridor, Paul said, "Is Jennifer okay in there with him?"

"Chiusolo's probably showing her pictures of his wife right now."

Paul said, "Man, the guy's a talker. It took me a while to get a word in edgewise. But no question he believes I'm a big time art collector."

"You're on your game. Nice touch with the Boston Rembrandt."

"For a second I thought I'd stepped in it. But yeah, thanks. I've definitely set the hook on *View of the Sea*."

"No offense, but he was in with both feet already when I called to invite him into the process. Relax and enjoy the rest of your dinner."

"Why didn't we bring him in earlier?"

"Because before we were trying to keep this quiet." When they got back from the men's room, Jennifer and Chiusolo were smiling and laughing with each other like old friends. As Mickey and Paul approached, she handed Chiusolo a compact mirror from her clutch, and he held it up and started smoothing his eyebrows. They were dark brown, bushy and unruly, running off in all directions.

"There, isn't that better?" Jennifer said.

"It's too dignified."

Jennifer laughed.

Chiusolo said, "And it ruins my trademark feature, part of my crazy-man image. I need these ratty bastards to help me strike fear in the hearts of my clients and worker bees."

He handed the compact back to Jennifer and ruffled his eyebrows again.

As Paul and Mickey sat back down, Chiusolo said to Mickey, "Jennifer's been trying to take some of the Jersey City boy out of me."

"Not possible," Mickey said.

"So where are we?" Chiusolo said.

"You're in," Paul said. "I'll let Mickey lay out the mechanics for you."

"We'll give you a time slot at 4 p.m. on Thursday. You'll be the last buyer to see the painting before final bids are due. Who are you using as your expert to verify it?"

"I use a guy named Franchetti."

Mickey nodded.

Chiusolo said, "Now I need to figure out where Georgianne will put it."

Jennifer said, "John's been telling me he wants to buy the painting for a major milestone birthday gift for his wife."

Chiusolo said, "I told Jennifer how our master bedroom and dressing room are laid out. She thinks putting it next to Georgianne's makeup table is a nice spot. That's a place where no one else goes, and Georgianne can admire it every time she gets dressed to go out."

As they got ready to leave the restaurant, Jennifer said goodbye and excused herself to use the ladies' room. Paul stood by the revolving door to see Chiusolo out, but Chiusolo pulled Mickey aside, yet still within earshot of Paul.

"A freakin' van Gogh! Wow! Georgianne's gonna flip. Don't let me down, bro. You're not an investment banker anymore. You don't have to worry about this 'level playing field' garbage. Tell me where I need to be and I'm there. What's this gonna take?"

"I can't tell you that."

Chiusolo looked at Mickey for a long moment, then said, "You can at least tell me if the number will have a two or three in front of it, can't you?"

Mickey glanced over at Paul. "I'm trying to do the best I can for my client."

"Let me know, bro. I'll make it up to you." Chiusolo's limo pulled up outside and he and Mickey headed for the revolving door.

Paul extended his hand as Chiusolo approached. "A pleasure to meet someone with common interests." He stood a full four or five inches taller than Chiusolo, smiling down on him, making solid eye contact as he shook his hand. "I'll be proud to know I sold you this special piece. It'll be in hands that appreciate it as much as it should be," he said, acting like the deal was clinched with a preemptive close.

After they were in a cab, Mickey said to Jennifer, "Did he show you pictures of Georgianne?"

"No, but he told me all about her. High school sweetheart, a year behind him in school. He the captain of the football team, she a cheerleader. He did have half a dozen photos of his new-born granddaughter, though. The poor girl has the biggest nose I've ever seen on any baby, ever. She'll have to get a nose job by the time she's 12 or she'll never survive high school. John kept telling me how beautiful she was, asking me if I agreed. It's hard not to like a man like that."

Mickey smiled.

"Is Georgianne attractive?" Paul asked.

Mickey nodded. "About five years ago when I was still jogging, I was running through Central Park one morning without my contacts in. Off in the distance I saw a couple walking together. I said to myself, 'Who's that shapely young blonde with that older man?' As I got closer I realized it was Georgianne and John. When I got to the office I called Chiusolo and told him the story. He laughed his butt off. I think I've heard him tell that story 10 times since then."

Jennifer said, "Let him down easy, please."

That night at about 11:30, Mickey had just pulled out the convertible sofa in the living room of Jennifer's apartment and slid under the covers when his phone rang. He looked at the screen but he wasn't wearing his glasses and couldn't read it, so he just answered, "Yes?"

"Mickey?"

It was Rachel. She was whispering, as if maybe she was in bed as well and didn't want to disturb anyone else.

He chuckled. "That's right. You called me, remember?"

"Oh hush up," she said. "How are you?"

"Good. Just getting into bed."

"Me too."

She was still whispering, a playful quality to it. He thought of asking her if she called to tuck him in, but decided it was inappropriate. Instead he said, "Nice to hear your voice. You doing okay?"

"You asked me to call you when I was going back to the apartment. McCaskey and his partner are picking me up at

7 tomorrow morning to bring me back. I realize it's late, but I didn't know if you'd be up that early and decided it was better to call tonight." After a brief pause, she added, downright coquettishly, "And I didn't want you to yell at me if I didn't call, Mr. Steinberg, because I promised I would." Mickey was beginning to wonder if maybe she'd had a couple of glasses of wine.

"Thank you. This sets my mind at ease."

"Thanks for your concern. I'm sure I'll be safe now."

"What kind of protection did McCaskey promise you this time?"

"The same. Two men downstairs at all times."

"That's it?" Mickey felt a flush of alarm. "That's ridiculous. What's Walter doing about that?"

"Walter? What's Walter got to do with it?"

"Everything. He's your fiancé. Your safety should be his primary concern. He should be intervening to make sure White doesn't get to you again."

"Is that so?" She wasn't whispering anymore, and her voice sounded tense.

Mickey felt a surge of annoyance. "Yes. Like hiring a bodyguard, for starters. Which is what I would do if I were in his place. And I told him so myself."

"You told him? When?" Now *she* was starting to sound annoyed.

"Yes, I told him, the day after you and I had that scare with White. And I gave Holden a piece of my mind as well, so I can't believe that Holden isn't having McCaskey put more men on you. But I'm flat-out astounded that Walter isn't doing anything at all." Mickey realized he'd raised his voice. His hands started to tremble with anger as he thought back on that conversation with Goldstein.

"You've overstepped," Rachel said. "You had no right to call Walter and berate him that way."

"Berate him? I was trying to point out to him what his responsibilities are to the woman he purports to love. For a man who presents himself as an Old World gentleman he seems to have very little concept of chivalry."

"Mickey—"

"I'm sorry. I'm sorry. Overstepping, I know." He made himself take a breath. "What matters is this: once you get there, you are under no circumstances to leave the apartment until this whole thing with White has been resolved."

"That's preposterous. I can't shut down my entire life because of this situation. But perhaps more important, you can't dictate to me how I should conduct myself. I think this conversation has been a mistake and we should say good night."

"I completely agree. Good night." Mickey hung up. He tossed the phone onto the coffee table and lay back down.

That didn't go so well.

———◆———

The next morning, Mickey said to Paul, "How many did you get?"

"Twelve, all black."

Mickey nodded, then asked, "Is Jennifer ready?"

"Almost." A few minutes later Jennifer walked out of the bedroom wearing a dark blue skirt and a green blazer over a white shirt. She carried a tweed blazer over her arm.

"Showtime," Mickey said. They went downstairs. Jennifer climbed into a black stretch limo waiting in front of the building.

"Good luck," Mickey said to her as she closed the door. Paul and he climbed into another waiting stretch limo.

Mickey figured that if Holden had his men watching, or if Goldstein was obsessive enough to try to have them followed to gauge the strength of the field of other bidders, they'd need to mix it up in good old New York fashion. They'd use a variant of the street-corner shell game where the scam artist had three walnut shells, hid the peanut under one of them, slid them around in front of the crowd and made someone pay $20 to guess which shell the peanut was under.

"What's your name?" Jennifer said to the limo driver.

"Mike."

"Hi, Mike. You know the itinerary?"

"Yes, ma'am. First pickup is at the Four Seasons Hotel, then we take a little tour around Manhattan, with a stop before the next hotel."

Mike pulled the limo up in front of the Four Seasons Hotel on 57th Street and Jennifer got out, walked inside and climbed the stairs into the seating area on the left side of the lobby. She looked around and spotted a dapper man with graying hair talking to a disheveled man seated next to him. Both men stood up as she approached. The stylish man said, "Are you Jennifer?"

Jennifer smiled and extended her hand. "Yes. Mr. Wynn?"

"Yes, and this is Mr. Bernoulli."

"Our car is waiting, gentlemen." She led them out the front door, where Mike stood holding the door open to the limo. Jennifer could see that their other black stretch limos had assumed their positions, two parked in front of Mike's car, two more behind. *Two shells in front, two behind.*

Jennifer got Wynn and Bernoulli settled in the limo and seated herself. *And I've got the peanut hidden in mine.* "Okay, Mike," she said. Mike waved his hand out the window and the two limos in front pulled out. Mike followed. Jennifer glanced behind her to see the other two limos fall in behind them. In a line, they turned north on Sixth Avenue, crossed 59th Street and entered the drive into Central Park, at one point Mike slowing his car to allow one of the limos behind to pass him. As they reached the middle of the park, they executed another maneuver and switched places again. Just before the light at 79th Street and Fifth Avenue they did another switch. Jennifer checked behind her as they pulled out from the light and turned down Fifth. *Nothing.* No unmarked Crown Victorias or Impalas following them, nothing else looking suspicious.

They drove downtown to 34th Street, crossed to First Avenue and then headed north. Still in a line, the five limos entered the First Avenue Tunnel at 42nd Street just before the UN Building. In the lead at that point, Mike stopped his limo behind another black stretch limo parked halfway up the tunnel between 42nd and 47th streets, its flashers blinking. When the rest of the convoy of limos passed, the parked limo pulled out and joined it. Mike kept their limo parked inside the tunnel. Bernoulli looked back and forth from Jennifer to Wynn. Wynn sat with his elbow on the armrest and his head cradled in his palm as if he did this every day.

Jennifer checked her watch, waited three minutes, then said, "Okay, Mike. Let's go." He pulled out, crossed town on 55th Street and drove down Lexington Avenue, stopping at the rear entrance to the Waldorf Astoria Hotel. Jennifer removed her green blazer and put on her tweed one. She said, "Alright, gentlemen. This way, please."

She led them into the hotel and to the Waldorf Towers elevator, then escorted them to the suite Mickey and Paul had rented. When she brought the men in, Mickey and Paul were seated in the living room of the suite with a tray of tea, chocolates and assorted cookies on the coffee table.

View of the Sea at Scheveningen stood on an easel behind them.

Paul watched as Jennifer, wearing a tweed blazer that made her look like a thoroughbred from a Polo Ralph Lauren catalog, brought in Wynn and his expert, Bernoulli, a balding guy with droopy eyes and eczema. Jennifer then folded her hands in front of her and stood by the door. Bernoulli didn't wait for any introductions, just walked immediately to the painting. Wynn's face exploded into a toothy smile of recognition. "Mickey!" he called, crossed the room and gave Mickey a handshake and a slap on the back, then turned to Paul.

Giving Wynn a smile as good as he got, Paul said, "Mr. Wynn, I presume," and stuck out his hand.

"And you must be Paul Hilton." Wynn looked him in the eye as they shook, and Paul almost had to force himself not to wince at the firmness of Wynn's grasp.

A no-nonsense guy.

Paul said, "Please, have a seat."

Wynn sat on the sofa with his back to the painting, Mickey in an armchair to one side, Paul in one on the other. Paul could see Bernoulli now examining the upper left corner of the painting with a magnifying glass.

Paul said, "Was your trip okay?"

Wynn nodded. "Sure. It's a snap with your own plane. Cuts out all the nonsense at the airport."

Paul smiled. "What do you fly?"

"Gulfstream G-5. You?"

"I charter. They give me something different each time, but the G-5 is a great plane." Paul smiled and winked at him. "Guys like me can actually stand up in them. More often I fly a Learjet 60XR because of its range. I'm based in Hong Kong."

"So I hear from Mickey."

Paul settled back and crossed his legs. "It's a pleasure to meet you. And I'm really glad to have you in the process."

"I'll bet you are. I'm told I've got a reputation for paying too much. Can you give me any idea who I'm bidding against?"

Paul laughed and looked at Mickey.

Mickey said, "Think of it as if you're bidding against yourself. That ought to really get you to pay up."

Wynn turned to smile at Mickey as he said it. When he did, Paul glanced up to see that Bernoulli was now examining the painting with a machine he removed from his briefcase, maybe a spectrograph, still focusing on the upper left. *Man, what's he doing?*

Wynn turned back to Paul. "I'm curious. Why sell?"

Paul leaned forward and put his elbows on his thighs, looking Wynn in the eye. "My collecting interests have evolved. I used to be like you, or at least my perception of how you collect—finding elite-quality jewels, the best of the best, agnostic as to the artist, the period, or school of art. Not like, say, Leonard Lauder with his total focus on collecting cubism over the last 40 years. So when I—"

Wynn cut in. "That was some donation to the Met, huh? They're valuing Lauder's collection at over $1 billion. Some 70 paintings, drawings and sculptures."

"Seventy-eight, to be exact," Paul said. "But as I was saying, I started out like you, which was how I chose to buy *View of the Sea*, a real prize. Around that time I bought a few Lichtensteins, a Turner, a Donatello, Rauschenbergs, Warhols, and even some Rembrandt sketches. Fabulous pieces, but I was all over the place. So over the last four or five years I've found myself focusing more and more on a few artists."

"So obviously van Gogh isn't one of them, then."

Mickey said, "But you do have some other van Goghs, don't you, Paul?"

Wynn turned to look at Mickey again, and Paul took another opportunity to glance over his shoulder at Bernoulli, who had his face up to *View of the Sea*, sniffing it.

"I do have some of his pen-and-ink drawings from his Hague series," Paul said.

"Hague series?" Wynn asked. "I'm not familiar with that."

"Early works," Paul said. "From 1882, the same year he painted *View of the Sea*. A series of 12 pen-and-ink drawings of the city, commissioned by his uncle Cornelis, who was an art dealer. His uncle dismissed them as without merit. Ironically, now they're considered great masterpieces by van Gogh collectors."

Mickey said, "And you've got how many of them, Paul?"

"Three, and I doubt I'd ever sell them."

Wynn said, "So you say you're focused on specific artists."

"That's right. Rauschenberg, Lichtenstein and Warhol, mostly. I find it more rewarding to get to know them as they evolve, watch the subtleties of their changes in technique. See their emotions translated into their expressiveness as they develop. Note how they distance themselves from their initial influences, then really dig into the parts of their souls that define their mature work."

"Wow. I'm impressed," Wynn said, widening his eyes and leaning back in his chair. "I just see stuff I like and buy it."

The three men laughed at that, then went on talking about other artists. At one point Paul caught a glimpse of Jennifer smirking as he carried on about Lichtenstein's work as if he—rather than she—had had his nose stuck in art history books for six years, and had actually viewed the paintings he was so effusive about.

After about 20 minutes Bernoulli turned from the painting, stepped over and tapped Wynn on the shoulder, smiling. Wynn nodded and then stood up to walk over and look at the painting. He stepped back and said, "I haven't seen you in about 15 years, but you're still a beauty," then turned around and smiled at Paul, then Mickey. They all shook hands and Jennifer escorted Wynn and Bernoulli out to take them downstairs to the limo and back to the Four Seasons.

Paul let out a sigh. *One down, five to go.*

———◦◇◦———

Back at Jennifer's apartment that evening, Paul's, Jennifer's and Mickey's spirits were high. They'd done meet-and-greets and viewings with Wynn, Geffen, Murdoch and Gates at the Waldorf, Sherry-Netherland, Peninsula and InterContinental hotels. Paul and Mickey moved from hotel to hotel without incident, enjoying a leisurely lunch in the Peninsula's excellent restaurant, Fives, and all of them getting home to Jennifer's apartment in time to enjoy a dinner of take-out Chinese.

"I never thought I'd get any use out of that ridiculous green blazer," Jennifer said.

Paul said, "Makes you look like you won the Masters."

"Golf. A game even more boring than that blazer. I thought I'd thrown it away years ago."

Mickey said, "All in all, a good day's work. No hiccups. No sign of Charlie Holden and his men. We're on our way. In a little over 24 hours, we should have this thing wrapped up and be ready to celebrate." Mickey was trying to pump himself up as much as the others, because he'd had a nervous flutter in his stomach all day.

After they finished dinner, Mickey went into the living room and picked up his cell phone. He was looking forward to this. He checked his watch: 6:15 p.m. Fifteen minutes later than he'd promised Goldstein he would call to give him his final instructions.

Goldstein picked up on the first ring.

"Walter, it's Mickey."

"I've been eagerly anticipating your call, old man."

"I know. It seems we've had some complications." He paused, waiting to see what Goldstein's tone was. Would he still be cocky, or would he now be concerned he was really in competition with other bidders? When Goldstein didn't respond, Mickey said, "We've had a new party enter the process and we're working hard to accommodate everyone. It seems given our compressed time frame that we'll need to change your 4 p.m. time slot tomorrow. We can give you either 2 p.m. or 7 p.m. Which would work for you?"

Mickey waited. Would Goldstein push back or accept the change?

Goldstein said, "Aside from it being downright rude, this last-minute alteration will be inconvenient at either time." He paused.

Mickey waited.

"I must tell you, old man, that this whole cloak-and-dagger skulduggery is beginning to wear a bit thin. It's quite . . . unsavory."

Still Mickey waited.

Goldstein exhaled heavily. "I suppose, given that you are insisting that final bids are due at 9 p.m., I prefer 2 p.m. But I must tell you that I am hopeful I won't need to be dealing with you on any more of these transactions in the future. I feel I should add that you don't seem to be any more competent with this process than you have been in securing Rachel's safety, in light of the fact that you have some crazed killer stalking her to get to you. I'm afraid this most recent incident two days ago almost succeeded in getting her killed."

Mickey's hands started to shake with a burst of anger. "Since you brought it up, I was thinking of telling you the same thing. If our situations were reversed, I either wouldn't let Rachel out of my sight, or would have hired a couple of bodyguards to accompany her wherever she went."

Mickey wanted to totally unleash on Goldstein, but forced himself to calm his breathing, relax his grip on the cell phone. He pulled the phone away from his ear for a moment, took a deep breath, exhaled. He said, "Back to business here. Are we confirmed at 2 p.m.?"

Goldstein said, his tone icy, "Yes. 2 p.m. Shall I expect your car at our apartment promptly, or will I be kept waiting, as I was for this call?"

"We'll pick you up at 1:30. If you aren't there, we'll go forward without you." Mickey hung up.

Mickey's first instinct was to throw his cell phone at the wall. He took a deep breath, let it out and then placed his cell phone on the coffee table in front of him. Then he smiled. Goldstein believed he wasn't alone in the process, couldn't call the shots. They were still in business.

Thursday morning, the final day of buyer meet-and-greets and viewings—bid day—Jennifer walked into the living room of her apartment with a cup of tea as Mickey picked up his cell phone. She wore pajama shorts and one of Paul's white shirts.

Mickey dialed Chiusolo's cell phone.

"John, it's Mickey. We need to talk."

"Oh, man, bro, I can hear it in your voice. You're gonna let me down, aren't you? Don't do this to me. I already told Georgianne I'm giving her a special painting for her birthday, one that will blow her socks off. I even showed her where I thought it should go in her dressing room."

"I'm going to have to disappoint you on *View of the Sea*. In retrospect, I should never have even called you about it, because we already had too many parties in the process."

Chiusolo was silent at the other end of the phone.

Mickey continued. "So it's just not going to happen for you."

Chiusolo still didn't respond.

"I'm sorry, maybe next time. I owe you one," Mickey said and hung up. He looked over at Jennifer.

She said, "I feel dirty."

Mickey nodded. "So do I."

It wasn't a strenuous day, with only two buyer meetings—Buffett and Goldstein—but when they returned to Jennifer's apartment in the afternoon, Mickey felt drained. He knew it was last-minute tension and anticipation with a bid deadline looming at 9 p.m. He'd been through it thousands of times on deals. It was probably also the nagging concern about Holden's men somehow showing up and intervening, or that crazy man Moravian White jumping from behind a parked car with a gun in his hand.

Paul was ebullient, like a young Associate working on his first major deal, smiling and cracking jokes with Jennifer as they rode up in the elevator. Mickey could sense Jennifer's excitement, too, all smiles. She hooked her arms through Paul's and Mickey's as they walked from the elevator to the door of her apartment. Once they were inside, Paul called out, "High five!" and raised his hand in the air for Mickey to slap it. Mickey did so, and Paul planted a kiss on Jennifer's lips.

Paul said, "I know it's too early for champagne, but I'm gonna put a bottle on ice."

"Stay inside yourselves," Mickey said. "It's not over yet."

"Come on, man. We're on the 18th green, three feet from the hole and even on strokes."

"Maybe, but the last thing we want to do is lose our concentration and yank the putt to lose the match."

Jennifer said, "You can keep yourself under control for all of us. I'm with Paul. I'm going to get some champagne flutes." She and Paul walked into the kitchen.

Mickey had to admit it had gone smoothly. Goldstein and he, as Mickey expected, behaved like gentlemen, as if their tense exchange of the previous day had never happened. Goldstein's visit to the suite they'd rented at the St. Regis for his viewing was brief, only 15 minutes. He'd engaged in five minutes of his usual social nonsense as foreplay, then viewed the painting. He'd used no tools or even a magnifying glass, as if those were beneath the mastery of his trained eyes. He'd turned back from the painting and said to Mickey, "A masterpiece. You'll have my response tonight by the appointed hour."

Then he left.

Mickey had scrutinized Goldstein carefully the entire time he was in the suite. He detected nothing to tell him that Goldstein didn't believe he was in a full-blown auction.

It was around 4 p.m. when Mickey got a phone call from Bernoulli. After he hung up he put the phone down on the arm of the chair next to him, his stomach beginning to churn. It must have showed in his face because Paul said, "What's wrong?"

"Bernoulli—Wynn and Buffett's expert—wants another look at the painting."

Paul walked over and sat down on the sofa across from Mickey. "That doesn't sound good."

"I don't know. I'll call Bouchard and get his advice."

It was difficult to get hold of anyone when calling into Yankton, so it wasn't until 5:15 that the message eventually got to Bouchard and he phoned back. Mickey put him on speaker for Jennifer and Paul.

"Oh, that Italian fool, grandstanding again," Bouchard said when Mickey told him about Bernoulli's request. "Still, it's not abnormal. I'd say it happens about 25% of the time. What you need to do is call all the other experts and arrange a group viewing, including our man, Scopes."

"Then what?" Mickey asked.

"Then stand back and watch the show. Sometimes it can be quite a spectacle. Imagine a half-dozen pompous, frustrated college professors, trying to one-up each other on how profoundly they bear the torch of artistic knowledge. Just make sure Scopes keeps his poise, because the group viewing presents a challenge to his certification, and, thus, his ego. There may be some hand-wringing, but it will all be over in an hour or less."

"Okay," Mickey said. "Then it shouldn't affect our bid deadline."

"That doesn't sound so bad," Paul said when they hung up.

Mickey smiled and nodded, but he wasn't convinced; he'd be out of his element, with little ability to control the meeting if things turned in the wrong direction.

Moravian White was a patient man, but he was getting tired of these subway rides, the L train from Canarsie to 14th Street in Manhattan, transfer to the No. 4, 5 or 6 train and up to 59th Street and then walk over to Park Avenue and 63rd to the Steinberg woman's apartment building, hang out across the street, walk around the block, whatever, still seeing the cops parked outside. He kept thinking about the Steinberg woman and how close he had come to Steinberg himself in Chelsea a few days ago. He knew it was still just a question of time.

Yeah, he was patient. Just like what he'd learned in the neighborhood, him and big brother Dontelle sitting on top of their apartment building, Moravian with the Daisy BB air rifle, Dontelle at his side with the pellet pistol, waiting for pigeons. When one showed up, Dontelle would always clunk off a few rounds with the pellet pistol, missing every time, and scare them off, Moravian telling himself, *they'll be back*, and waiting, the Daisy resting across his lap. Usually it was a single pigeon that came back after Dontelle fired his wild rounds, and Moravian would tap Dontelle on the shoulder, say, "My turn," then put his finger to his lips and take aim with the Daisy. Sometimes he'd wait two or three minutes, setting it up, waiting for the pigeon to stop twitching and bobbing its head before he'd shoot, plugging it off the ledge 95% of the time.

Now he had to be just as patient, hanging out across the street on Park Avenue in his hoodie, waiting for the Steinberg woman. He knew the Chelsea Hotel was a dead end. Seeing Steinberg run as fast as he did while Moravian chased him, he knew the little Jew would never come back to the Chelsea again.

Mickey reserved a suite at the Pierre hotel for a group viewing at 7 p.m. and then called the four experts and their man, Scopes, all of whom were aware they were on call until after bids were due. Paul arranged for the convoy of limousines again while Jennifer went into the bedroom to change back into what she now called her "chaperone suit."

Mickey and Paul got into their limo, went through the shell game with their escorting limos and eventually arrived at the

Pierre, while Jennifer did her routine with her fleet of limousines as well.

When Jennifer escorted the five men into the suite at the Pierre, Mickey could see instantly that Scopes' face was drawn, his pointed nose seemingly even more pointed, and his jaw clenched with tension. Mickey and Paul stood up when they entered, trying to appear as relaxed as possible, knowing that if dogs could smell fear, maybe art historians could, too. Bernoulli, a sad sack in a rumpled herringbone, went directly to *View of the Sea* and began inspecting the upper left quadrant of it from inches away.

Mickey waved Scopes over to the corner to speak to him. "Any discussion in the limo?"

"Nothing. Bernoulli didn't say a word beyond 'hello.' Sloan, Prentice and Stilton were chatting about nothing in particular. Seems they're fairly relaxed and have just come along for the ride." Scopes was speaking rapidly, clipping his words as if biting off the ends of them, clearly angry, the strain in his voice evident. "It's Bernoulli. But then, it's usually Bernoulli with one of these things."

"He's done this before?"

"Oh, yes. And nine times out of 10 it's to me, when I'm representing the seller as the one who certifies the painting."

Mickey nodded, hoping this was just a rivalry between academics playing itself out.

"I'm going over there," Scopes said.

"Give him his space," Mickey said. "No sense rushing the man."

Scopes walked over and sat down on a chair adjacent to the sofa. At that point Bernoulli turned around and motioned to one of the other three experts, who had seated themselves on the sofa. The man walked over and Bernoulli pointed to something in the sky in the upper left of the painting. They talked for a few moments and then the man walked back over and sat down. Mickey saw the man shrug at Scopes and then go back to conversing with the other two experts.

Paul took out his cell phone and made a call, or an imaginary one to appear nonchalant. He walked over and stood by the door, talking and pacing slowly back and forth in front of Jennifer, not paying any attention to her as if he didn't know her.

After another ten minutes, Bernoulli turned around to face the group and said, as if addressing a classroom of undergraduate students, "I'm having a real problem here. It's not just the cloud formation Gabriel, but Neptune as well."

Scopes stood up and addressed him from across the room. "And what is your concern?"

"If you gentlemen will be so kind as to come over, I'll show you." The five men converged and stood hunched around the painting, Bernoulli pointing to the sky in the upper left, then to the center of the painting near the mast of the fishing boat.

After a moment Scopes strode over to Mickey, breathing heavily, his nostrils flaring, and said, "We in the art world affectionately refer to shapes that appear to be 'faces' in the cloud formations as Gabriel and Neptune. There's been a long-running controversy in art circles about whether or not van Gogh intended for his brushstrokes to depict faces, but even the uninitiated can see them once they're pointed out. Gabriel, in the upper left, is a clear rendition of a face, appearing to be attached to a winged horse, with a long trumpet extending in front of him, hence the name 'Gabriel.' Neptune appears to be another face with puffed cheeks, blowing at the fishing boat from just to the right of the flag on its mast."

"So what's his concern?"

Scopes' voice went up in pitch. "Bernoulli says they're too pronounced, that they look artificially enhanced, so that he can't certify the painting is genuine to his buyers."

Paul had now hung up from his call, whether imaginary or real, and walked over. "Just what's going on here?" he said, sounding indignant.

Mickey held his hand out to him to cut him off. "Has this ever happened before?" Mickey said.

Scopes said, "Only when the painting is a forgery, to my knowledge."

Scopes looked at Paul, who threw his head back as if he were insulted.

"What about the other experts?" Mickey said.

"I've protested." Scopes was now sputtering. "Since I'm an authority on the subject—in fact I've written a paper on it entitled '*The Faces of Scheveningen*'—but Bernoulli isn't budging. I don't know if the others will fall in line behind Bernoulli or me."

Mickey felt the strength draining from his legs, sensed his chest sagging. He'd been here before. One buyer uncovers a huge environmental hazard or shaky patents in his due diligence, pulls out of the process and it cascades from there. Word gets out and all the buyers disappear. Busted deal, end of story.

At that moment, Bernoulli walked over to the front door of the suite. He turned and said, "Gentlemen, thank you for your courtesy over the last days, and for the opportunity to participate in your process. But I'm leaving, and I cannot advise my clients to proceed with the purchase. I wish you the best." He turned, opened the door and left.

The other three experts looked at each other, then over at Scopes, and made for the door as if someone had thrown a grenade into the room.

Scopes said to Mickey, "I'm sorry," and then to Paul, "good luck."

Mickey walked over and slumped onto the sofa, feeling dead inside. He looked over at the painting, the painting that was to have been his first step out of the mess that currently constituted his life. Broke, no friends, no job, no prospects, no future. He'd lost Rachel and didn't see any way to get her back. He couldn't even pay her back the $20 thousand she'd lent him. Worst of all, he'd been unable to crush Goldstein. The fraud had conned Rachel out of her money and was probably spending it cheating on her with other women.

Mickey felt like he'd be better off getting hit by a bus.

Paul and Jennifer walked over and sat down across from him. Paul's face was ashen. Jennifer's eyes were sympathetic.

Paul said, "Now what?"

"Stick a fork in us. We're cooked," Mickey said.

CHAPTER 6

They rode the limo back to Jennifer's apartment. When they got there Mickey stood the painting up on the seat of a chair. He sat down on the sofa and just stared at it. Paul and Jennifer walked into the kitchen. He could hear them whispering to each other in there. He wondered if they thought he was depressed and might do something crazy, like go out in the street and start yelling, "Hey, White. Moravian White. Here I am, come and get me." Then their whispering grew louder. One of them closed the kitchen door and he heard them talking, then arguing loudly. He couldn't make out anything they were saying, but it went on for a while.

When Paul and Jennifer came back in and sat down across the coffee table from him, they both looked angry.

Mickey said, "Bouchard must've overlooked the details in those cloud formations."

Paul said, "It doesn't seem possible. I watched him in his room as he copied the painting, using those tiny projected grids he set up, like Scopes did when he verified it. Bouchard went over each little grid like a Swiss watchmaker."

Mickey checked his watch. It was almost 9:00 p.m. "We'll have a chance to talk to him about it shortly," Mickey said. "Bouchard's probably pacing around in his room right now, eager to know where the bids came in."

They sat in silence for a moment, then Paul said, "What if we go back to Chiusolo?"

Jennifer glared at him. "I can't believe you're going to actually suggest this."

Paul ignored her. "What do you think, Mickey?"

Mickey glanced at Jennifer, then made eye contact again with Paul. "If he hasn't already heard it's a fake, he'd find out by talking to his expert shortly after we called him."

Jennifer threw her head back in her chair. She snapped at Mickey, "So you're considering it? I thought you said this was about Goldstein."

"It is. Or was."

"So why would you even entertain the idea of trying to take advantage of John Chiusolo?"

"I'm not. I was only answering Paul's question. It's all academic at this point. Nobody's going to buy the thing." He glanced over at the painting.

"I'm not so sure," Paul said. "All the experts verified it at first. What if we got Scopes back in, paid him more and got him to stand behind it with Chiusolo?"

Jennifer said, "I can't believe I'm hearing this."

Paul said to her, "We're just considering our options here. Why can't you do that without flying off the handle?" He turned back to Mickey, said, "What do you think about Chiusolo?"

"What are you, a crook?" Jennifer said to Paul.

Paul turned to her again. "Yeah, I guess so. I went to jail for being part of a crooked securities firm, remember? I hate to tell you, babe, I'm not as squeaky clean as I led you to believe. And as you know, our partner in this deal, Mickey, isn't squeaky clean at all. His insider trading scheme netted billions before the Feds shut them down. And the three of us have been working a scam to try to get Goldstein to pay us $40 million for a fake painting. So don't get all self-righteous on me. We're *all* crooks, including *you*, babe. What's the difference if we scam Goldstein or Chiusolo? Are we going to salvage something out of this fiasco or not?"

"I can't listen to any more of this," Jennifer said and jumped to her feet. She strode into the bedroom and slammed the door.

"Don't worry about her, man. She'll cool off," Paul said. "Hear me out. I don't think Chiusolo gives a damn if the painting's fake, as long as his wife doesn't find out, and as long as there's no certainty one way or the other and he doesn't get publicly embarrassed for buying it. Maybe it's real, maybe it isn't. He'd still pay big bucks for it to be able to tell his wife he's bought her a van Gogh. You call Chiusolo and tell him the game's changed, he's in if he wants to be."

"What do I tell him when he talks to his expert and finds out everybody knows it's fake?"

"It's just Bernoulli. You saw yourself, all the other guys were fine with it until Bernoulli blew the whistle. Insist Chiusolo have his expert meet with Scopes to verify the painting."

At that moment Mickey's cell phone rang. He checked the time: 9:05. The caller ID was from Yankton. "It's Bouchard," Mickey said. He put the phone on speaker and rested it on the coffee table.

Mickey told Bouchard what had happened. While he was doing so, Paul walked over and opened the bedroom door. He came back a minute later with Jennifer, who sat down, her face still lined with tension.

"This is an outrage!" Bouchard yelled through the phone. "An absolute outrage!"

Mickey started to say something but Bouchard talked over him, his voice going up an octave, now shrieking like a cat. "No bona fide van Gogh expert would make such a comment. That ass, Bernoulli, was probably working from a second-rate print that softened the pixels and toned down the sharpness of the Gabriel and Neptune cloud clusters. He's an ass! An Italian ass! I worked and reworked those two sections of the painting at least a half-dozen times to make them perfect." Bouchard was calming down now, lowering his voice to a normal tone. "I used 10 times magnification on both my original print and the painting for those two sections. I could understand an expert protesting that the curl of the waves breaking in the center of the painting or the lines of the mast of the fishing boat are slightly sharper than the originals, but I absolutely, positively cannot understand how anyone, even an ass such as Bernoulli, could make such a comment in all honesty."

Mickey sat up straight on the sofa.

Bouchard went on. "Bernoulli has seen the painting. Years ago I stood next to him in Amsterdam and we viewed it together. We discussed it at length. This is a travesty."

Mickey leaned forward and asked, "How well do Bernoulli and Goldstein know each other?"

"As well as everyone knows each other among the experts and dealers in this strange and beautiful and sometimes darkly devious world. I believe the expression is 'thick as thieves.'"

Mickey looked over at Paul, then at Jennifer, and said, "Goldstein. It has to be Goldstein. When he couldn't queer the process by tipping off Holden, he paid off Bernoulli to blow it up."

Bouchard said, "An entirely plausible explanation."

Paul said, "This guy, Goldstein, is like dog shit. You step in it and you can never get it off your shoe."

Mickey said to Paul, "How long do you think it will be before I get a call from Goldstein offering us 10 cents on the dollar from his previous offer?"

Paul said, "Why would he offer us anything for a fake painting?"

Jennifer laughed in his face. "Because he thinks it's real, dufus."

Mickey smiled. "We're still alive."

———◆———

Later that evening Paul walked into the living room with a glass of burgundy. Mickey was counting a pile of money on the coffee table. He heard Paul and looked up, glanced at the wine glass and said, "Take it easy with that. You're on again soon, and this may be our last shot."

"I just poured it and I'm only having one glass. Don't worry about it. Keeps me in character." Paul shifted his feet, then said, "Something's been bothering me."

Mickey stopped counting and looked up to give Paul his attention.

"It's Goldstein. Something doesn't check out."

Mickey smiled. "That's not news to me. I've said all along the man's a fraud."

"Yeah, but you did your due diligence and ran into a dead end, right?"

"Essentially, yes."

"I've got some old friends who are still cops in LA. I'm going to make some calls and ask for some favors, see what they can dig up."

Mickey nodded and went back to his counting.

Paul walked over and sat down on the sofa next to Mickey as he finished. "How are we doing?"

Mickey wrote down a number on the back of the envelope, then stuffed the bills back inside. "We're running on vapors. We've only got $2,652 left. If we don't pull this off in the next round, we'll have to hock some of your suits."

"I'm sure you'll figure something out. You always do."

"I'm used to thinking my way around problems on deals, but I'm beginning to wonder if this one isn't going to get the better of me."

Paul smiled. "You're supposed to be the one with a cool head. Don't lose it or we'll *all* fall to pieces."

Mickey looked at Paul for a long moment, then reached out and took the glass of wine from him. He took a long sip.

Paul stood up. "Keep it; I'll get another," he said and walked back into the kitchen.

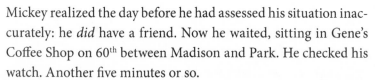

Mickey realized the day before he had assessed his situation inaccurately: he *did* have a friend. Now he waited, sitting in Gene's Coffee Shop on 60th between Madison and Park. He checked his watch. Another five minutes or so.

Mickey had a booth for two across from the counter, behind which was the chef's station. The place was a comfortable mix of the clang of spatulas on the grill, sizzling food, the aromas of steak, green peppers and onions and all manner of accents—Spanish, Asian, Indian and Greek—as orders were shouted, acknowledged, and busboys chewed out.

Hector walked in. Mickey waved, Hector seeing and acknowledging him with a smile. Mickey had to slide out sideways from under the table in the booth to be able to stand to shake Hector's hand when he reached the table.

"How you doin', man?" Hector said, pumping Mickey's hand.

"I've been around, working a few things," Mickey said. They sat down.

Hector said, "What you been up to?"

"You really want to know?"

Hector nodded.

Mickey told him the whole story about the painting, from the beginning. About wanting to find a talker at Yankton, meeting Paul, his idea for a deal, Bouchard, the painting, Goldstein, the auction, everything and everything in between, then Bernoulli blowing it all up in the suite in the Pierre. After he finished, Hector just stared at him for a few moments, Mickey wondering if Hector expected him to go on. Then Hector threw his head back and laughed out loud, to the point where patrons at the counter turned around, wondering what was going on. Hector took a sip of water, almost choked on it, coughed a few times and then said, "Man, when you do it, you do it up big, Mick. So now what?"

"I'm not sure. I remember something one of the guards at Yankton said, this big man named Sly, who was as dumb as a stone but managed to capture a simple wisdom at times. He said, 'A man's nothing if he's got to settle for being a has-been nobody the rest of his life.' I guess if things don't work out in the endgame of this painting deal, that's the reality I'm going to face. And I don't mind saying it's not a place I ever expected to be."

Mickey saw Hector scrutinizing him. Hector said, "You don't really believe that, do you? I mean, what's this stupid painting gonna do for you anyhow?"

"Get Rachel back. Nail Goldstein. Maybe even get some or all of my money back."

"If you're really gonna get Rachel back, I don't see how the painting makes much difference one way or the other. Sounds like it would be nice to nail Goldstein, but based on how he's living, he'll get his in the end anyhow."

"Scuzbags don't always get their due. Trust me, I know lots of corporate and Wall Street slime who've never gotten their comeuppance. It doesn't happen spontaneously. Somebody's got to start the process along, make sure it comes to pass."

"So what are you gonna do?"

"I'm not sure. I still haven't heard from Goldstein since the Bernoulli debacle."

"You called him yet?"

Mickey sighed, then smiled. "No, but I will eventually if he doesn't call me. But that would be an expensive phone call."

"But he knows your sale process has been ruined already, so what do you lose by calling him first?"

Mickey had to hand it to Hector. For a man who'd spent his life as a concierge, he was pretty savvy about the ins and outs of deals. He bet Hector drove a pretty hard bargain buying a car. Mickey said, "Yes, but he doesn't know what we're thinking, what we're up to."

"So what *are* you up to?"

Mickey smiled. "I'm still not sure, but as I told you, Paul pointed out our only other option last night. Chiusolo."

Hector cocked his head. "You're not gonna screw this guy, Chiusolo, are you? Sell him the painting? You said you like the guy."

Mickey had a sinking feeling as he got ready to answer, once more hearing Sly's comment to him at Yankton, then feeling the tug of something else when he saw in his mind's eye Chiusolo's excitement at the door to Le Bernardin, saying "A freakin' van Gogh!" Mickey looked Hector in the eye for a long moment, then said, "I'd be lying if I told you I hadn't thought about it. But I can't do it. This thing has always been about Goldstein."

Hector said, "And Rachel."

"Yes, and Rachel. But it doesn't keep me from using Chiusolo as a shill for Goldstein if that's all we've got going for us."

"Yeah, but you'll sure be jerking the guy around."

"He's a big boy. Plus, he'll know I'll owe him one and someday I'll make it up to him."

Hector thought for a moment. "You said, 'If that's all we've got going for us,' like you're feeling down on your luck. But Goldstein still thinks the painting's real, right?"

Mickey nodded.

"Seems to me that's a lot to have going for you."

Goldstein called Mickey while Hector was paying the check—Hector had insisted on paying, and as he did so Mickey gathered it was Hector's regular place, because the short Mexican kid behind the register called him "Mr. Hector, sir."

On the phone, Goldstein sounded as obsequious as ever, oozing sympathy for Mickey over his broken deal and offering, "Dinner on him, in the real New York," to discuss an idea Goldstein had to help out with Mickey's situation.

Hector smiled as Mickey repeated the phone conversation as he walked Hector back to 465 Park. As Mickey shook Hector's hand before he entered the building, Hector said, "I told you once before, Mick, you're better'n all these guys, because you've never looked down your nose on anybody. Let me know how your deal turns out. And come out to Park Slope for dinner anytime. Maria would love to see you."

———◆———

Back at Jennifer's apartment that afternoon, Mickey's cell phone rang. He looked at the screen: RACHEL. He felt his pulse pick up.

"Rachel. What a nice surprise."

"I thought I'd check in." She paused. "I hadn't heard from you in a while, and I just wanted to make sure you're . . . alright."

Mickey said, "I'm doing fine."

"Nothing from the Caribbean man?"

"No. Has he bothered you again?"

Rachel said, "No. Holden's office still has people stationed downstairs at our apartment building." She paused again. "About that, Mickey."

"About what?"

"The last time we spoke. I flew off the handle."

"And I overstepped. Though frankly, I'd do it again. I can't help worrying about you."

Rachel didn't respond right away. Mickey sensed his own awkwardness now, the two of them tentative, feeling each other out. He felt a quaver of emotion in his chest, then hunched over and lowered his voice, as if this was a private moment he didn't want anyone to overhear, even though no one else was in the room. He said, "I thought of you today. I had lunch with Hector in a coffee shop. I was sitting in a booth waiting for him and it reminded me of sitting in Eisenberg's Sandwich Shop down on

Fifth Avenue, where we'd have lunch when you were working for Macmillan in the Flatiron Building. Remember?"

"Of course. When we were first dating." Her voice now had an airy quality to it.

"The place smelled like pastrami, dark mustard, and kosher pickles," he said. "The waiters would be bustling back and forth, weaving in and out of the tables."

"They had the thickest Brooklyn Jewish accents I've ever heard. They'd call out their orders from halfway across the floor, and the cooks would yell back to acknowledge them." Now he could hear Rachel chuckling softly.

"I'd wait in the booth watching the entrance for you to arrive," he said. "You'd keep me waiting sometimes." Neither of them said anything for a long moment until he added, "Then you'd walk in and smile at me, and I'd forget I was angry."

Rachel didn't respond.

Mickey felt a lump in his throat. He said, "Those were the days."

"Yes, they were," Rachel said in a whisper.

Mickey walked into the canopied entrance on 52nd Street to the Four Seasons restaurant for the first time in over three years, never daring to go into the place again after the announcement of his indictment. He left his topcoat at the checkroom and walked up the stairs. He entered the Front Bar and stepped into the glittering dance of light off the sculpture of bronze rods suspended over the bar, and the buzz of New York's most noteworthy chatting each other up, where he waited on a stool for Goldstein. After Goldstein arrived they had a quick drink, Mickey a Perrier with lime, Goldstein a glass of Bordeaux that he admitted was "still in its adolescence, although it will show its character with age," and at 7 p.m. were walked by a waif in a gold, shimmering top into the Pool Room for dinner.

Mickey followed the girl and Goldstein, on the way recognizing Stan Fischel, Mark Bantry and Stephen Forrestal seated at a table against the white marble pool and underneath one of the potted cherry trees. He made brief eye contact with Buck Howard, who averted his eyes. The place was as alive as ever with middle-aged captains of the universe in their tailored suits, their perfectly coifed wives or mistresses at their elbows, and animated with the chatter, energy and pulse of New York power, all framed against the lights of midtown Manhattan gleaming in through the floor-to-ceiling windows.

Mickey had girded himself for a long evening. Goldstein usually spent 20 to 30 minutes on foreplay on any subject, warming up to it with supercilious politeness before getting to the point. Mickey had resolved to pace himself, stay patient, even take some amusement from it.

So he was surprised when almost immediately after they sat down, and even before they'd been handed menus, Goldstein got right to it. "As I said earlier on the phone, I've been thinking about your situation and I'd like to propose a solution."

"My situation?"

"Yes, old man. Part of the reason why I suggested we dine here. Don't get me wrong, I think the food's quite good, but isn't the Four Seasons really a place to be seen rather than to dine?"

"What are you getting at?"

"My point is, I'm sure at least 20 prominent industrialists, lawyers and financial people will be on the phone tomorrow saying they saw us here together. I don't flatter myself that I'm that noticeable—"

Mickey was certain that he did.

"—but the delicious scandal of Mickey Steinberg having dinner with Walter Goldstein, the man who is to wed his former wife, no less, at such a prominent place certainly speaks of some storied transaction with millions involved. One in which everyone will want to be included."

Mickey couldn't help smiling, wondering where this bizarre mind in front of him intended to take him.

Goldstein continued. "So here are the facts. I'm a prominent art dealer connected with wealthy collectors on at least five continents, a unique position if I do say so myself." Goldstein allowed himself a pause and a sip of his adolescent Bordeaux. "You are one of the most celebrated financiers of our generation, recently even more famous because of the grand scale of the scandalous web you wove in engineering the most diabolically clever insider trading scheme in history. At the same time, you, through your young client, possess a painting that any art collector in the world knows is a cherished masterpiece that may never be seen again, at least legitimately." Goldstein had steepled his hands in front of him with his elbows on the table.

He continued, saying, "With that confluence of facts, what to do?" and raised his hands above his head as if saying "Hallelujah," in a charismatic Christian service.

"So you know the painting's real despite what Bernoulli said yesterday?"

Goldstein picked up his glass of wine again, took a sip and said evenly, "Of course, old man."

For a moment Mickey started to get angry. Then he realized that was dumb. *Stay inside yourself.* He waited a moment before saying, "So you said you have a proposal."

"In a nutshell, your asset is terribly compromised in your current position. We could combine your asset with the world-wide scope of my contacts and the considerable prestige of my reputation in the art world. My support would offset the unfortunate Mr. Bernoulli's uneducated faux pas in loudly declaring the painting a forgery, and could produce a result that would satisfy both of us, and certainly vastly exceed what your expectations might otherwise be in the current environment." Goldstein maintained eye contact with Mickey, adding for emphasis, "Which is to say, nothing."

Mickey said, "I'm still looking for the proposal in all this."

Goldstein said, "I propose a wholesale-to-retail strategy to sell the painting. You and I team up as co-wholesalers on the transaction. We use my broad range of contacts to increase the network of potential buyers, and of course include any of those you recently contacted, and then once we have our retail buyer, we take a wholesale margin—50% of the sale price—before we give the net to your young client, Paul. You and I would be partners on the wholesale transaction, 67% to me and 33% to you. I would not presume to share in whatever commission arrangement you might have with Paul."

"Let me get this straight. You're proposing that we go out together to sell the painting, then offer Paul half of what we get for it. So, if for example we get $40 million, we give Paul $20 million, and then you and I split the $20 million spread—your wholesale-to-retail—two thirds, one third, right?"

Goldstein smiled as if he could hardly contain himself with the brilliance of his plan. "You've got it spot-on, old man."

At that moment the waiter walked up with menus. Mickey said, "How about we put in our orders, get it out of the way so we can talk uninterrupted."

Mickey pretended to scan the menu but he didn't care what he ate. He figured if Goldstein's normal modus operandi was 20 to 30 minutes of pitter-patter before getting to the point, Mickey could do the same. Mickey ordered the beet salad with burrata as an appetizer and the Dover sole for the main course. Goldstein ordered the bouillabaisse and the double sirloin steak with béarnaise.

After they ordered, Mickey folded his hands and started talking about John Bell's offer to take his real estate company private, what he'd heard about how difficult the financing would be and how the commercial bankers at Bank of America were pulling their hair out about it. It was all made up, but it allowed Mickey to go on for about 10 minutes until he exhausted his imagination. Then he brought up Mayor Green's troubles with the Board of Education and the New York City Council over the new Superintendent of Schools he'd proposed, Claire Dixon, because it was the last thing Mickey had read in the *New York Times* before coming over to dinner. The *Times* reporter had written one of their usual excruciatingly long articles, and that gave Mickey material until halfway through the main course before he decided it was time to get around to it.

"I guess I should respond to your proposal," Mickey said.

Goldstein stopped chewing and looked up from his steak, his eyebrows raised expectantly.

"You're suggesting that I go around the back of my client and give him only 50% of what he would be entitled to in the sale transaction, and this without disclosing it to him."

Goldstein started chewing again, as if to empty his mouth and respond before Mickey could go any further.

"And that on top of the fact that you had offered to preempt our process at what I must admit is a healthy number, but a number I'm sure you wouldn't have stuck to if we agreed to allow you to preempt. I've seen that movie before. The selling advisor shuts down the sale process, tells all his other prospective buyers to go away, and the party who was to preempt starts waffling and his offer goes down to the point where the seller is either forced to go back to the other bidders with his hat in his hand or accept the lower price."

"See here, Mickey—"

"So when I called you after we had cocktails together and said we weren't going to allow you to preempt, something strange happened. I got a mysterious phone call summoning me to a meeting with Charlie Holden at the U.S. Attorney's Office, who told me he heard through the grapevine the full details of our auction process to sell a famous stolen painting. Don't you think it's a little coincidental that somebody just happened to tip off the Assistant U.S. Attorney in New York about what Paul and I were up to?"

"Surely you're not suggesting—"

"And then we decided to proceed on a fast track with a limited group of buyers so we wouldn't have to worry about Holden, and we were on the verge of doing a deal when you bribed Bernoulli to sabotage our process. That left you to call me and try to pick us off. So your strategy in this dinner is because you obviously decided that it was better to have me as an ally than an adversary, since I've outsmarted you twice already, and so you proposed this unethical scheme to get me in bed with you to betray my client."

By now Goldstein's face was almost as red as the interior of his steak. Mickey could see him working hard to hold himself in check, not wanting to make a scene in the middle of the Four Seasons Pool Room. He said in a loud whisper, "I must say this is incredibly ungracious and ungrateful of you, old man. I propose a way for you and your young client to dig yourself out of a terrible mess and salvage an unsalvageable situation by offering you the considerable weight of my prestige and contacts in the art world. And you sit here and insult me with a series of fantasies about how I've tried to do you wrong."

"I had already figured everything out, but you gave yourself away earlier when you mentioned Bernoulli."

Goldstein arched his head back, looking genuinely surprised.

"You said Bernoulli committed his faux pas by loudly declaring that the painting was a fake. He never said that. He just said he couldn't certify it."

Goldstein let out a breath and settled back into his chair, the anger gone from his face, as if he'd resigned himself to the fact that he'd been caught.

"How much did you pay Bernoulli?" Mickey asked.

Goldstein didn't respond.

"My interest is purely academic, in case I need to know for the future what the going rate is to bribe an art historian."

Goldstein lowered his gaze from Mickey to his double sirloin and began eating again.

Mickey went on. "So tell me, who is the buyer you've got lined up that allowed you to be bold enough to try to preempt, and then after that stay in the process? A Saudi prince? Some wealthy industrialist from Singapore? So you pay $30 or $40 million, and then lay off the painting on him for $50 million, maybe even $80 million?"

Now Goldstein looked up from his steak and said, "You should be careful. If you continue, I might very well make things difficult for you with the U.S. Attorney's Office."

"Again, you mean."

Goldstein looked Mickey in the eye. "Yes, again. So whatever your plans are, don't consider excluding me or I *will* make your life difficult. And since you're unwilling to accept my proposal, then you should at least accept the fact that you are in an impossible position." Goldstein put a substantial chunk of his steak in his mouth and chewed as he said through it, "You'll take whatever I offer you for the painting to get this over with. Let's be candid, you've no other choice."

Mickey said, "That's ridiculous. You and I both know the painting is authentic. If you want to buy it, you'll have to pay up. Otherwise I regroup, sort this out and start over again with my full group of bidders in a month, maybe six months. Even a year if I have to wait that long."

Goldstein snorted and sneered at him. "I'll offer you $4 million."

"You just don't get it. I already have a buyer in my pocket who's dying to have the painting. In an auction, it only takes one buyer. And if you already have him, it only takes one other to keep him honest. So now you're at $4 million, down from $40 million. But with real competition, where are you?"

"Five million dollars is my top offer. I'm certain none of your previous buyers will touch this thing after Mr. Bernoulli's performance."

"John Chiusolo."

Goldstein's eyes narrowed. "Need I remind you again about the U.S. Attorney's Office?"

Now Mickey leaned forward and put his elbows on the table, staring directly into Goldstein's eyes. "You're wearing out that threat. But here's a threat of my own. I can remember, as far back as that UJA-Federation dinner at the Waldorf, you getting into my ear about the rumors you were hearing about insider trading at Walker, and then going over and working Rachel. I saw it, but didn't put it together until later that you were making a move on her."

"You're getting rather pathetic, old man, bringing up Rachel. Jealousy isn't something I would have expected of you."

Mickey continued as if Goldstein hadn't spoken. "I've got this friend who's an ex-cop, and they have access to resources through other active cop friends of theirs that none of the rest of us do. This friend had his friends do some research on you. How about I tell Rachel about what he found out? Or maybe even tell the U.S. Attorney's Office. Werner Goldfarb. From a small town called Morges in Switzerland. Goldfarb, an upwardly mobile fellow. Married Gloria Stein, a rich young widow, then divorced her to move up to Francine Dreyfus in France. And so on. I don't really know how many times you've done it, but I know you were working the same routine when you came to the U.S. Taking advantage of women who are dumb enough, or vain enough, to fall for your phony European panache. Who are you, really, anyhow, old man? There's an old expression on Wall Street: 'Don't bullshit a bullshitter.' And remember, I'm a world-class bullshitter. A man who put together a $2 billion insider trading scam."

Mickey pushed his chair back. "Thanks for dinner. It's nice to get out again once in a while to the old haunts. We're going forward with the sale of the painting with however many parties are interested in participating, even if it's only Chiusolo. I'm thinking of tomorrow as the day to make it happen. Let me know if you're interested. If I don't hear from you by 10 a.m. tomorrow, I'll assume you're out." Mickey put his napkin on the table and stood up.

"I'm in," Goldstein said through clenched teeth.

"Okay. I'll be in touch later tonight."

Mickey started across the dining room. He pulled out his cell phone and dialed Paul. "We're going to need a dozen limos for tomorrow." For the first time since returning to New York he felt like he was back in form. He held his chin high and smiled as he weaved through the tables, not giving a damn about Goldstein's prediction that about 20 people would be on the phone the next day after seeing Mickey at the Four Seasons again, working on some deal. It was enough for him to know that he was.

The next morning the routine was the same as with the previous buyer viewings. Once Jennifer was ready, Paul, Jennifer and Mickey rode the elevator downstairs, Jennifer getting into one limo, Paul and Mickey the other. Paul and Mickey went to the Royalton Hotel and picked up John Chiusolo and Franchetti, his expert. They left the Royalton escorted by four other black stretch limos, did their exchange in the First Avenue Tunnel, and then proceeded to the Mandarin Oriental hotel. They waited in the limo and chatted with Chiusolo until they saw Jennifer's limo pull up with Goldstein in it.

Then Mickey nodded to Paul and they got out, bringing Chiusolo to the entrance just as Jennifer was getting out with Goldstein, making certain it was impossible for Goldstein not to see Chiusolo walking into the hotel. As Chiusolo recognized Goldstein, he turned back to Mickey and smiled. He said, "Here we go, bro." When they got upstairs, they put Chiusolo in a suite, and Jennifer put Goldstein in the suite next to his.

They crossed the hall and entered their own suite. Once inside, Jennifer handed Mickey Goldstein's cell phone. "He gave it up with no argument."

Mickey took it and put it on an end table next to Chiusolo's and the phones they'd unplugged from the two suites.

Paul took the painting out of a black portfolio case and set it up on a portable easel that Jennifer unfolded from her briefcase.

Paul said, "Okay, are we ready?"

Mickey said, "Let's let them sit for 15 or 20 minutes, build some tension."

After about 20 minutes, Mickey stood up, said, "Okay," and walked across the hall.

Mickey knocked on the door to Goldstein's suite and Goldstein opened the door, smiling and cordial as ever, as if there had never been any tension between them. "I'm ready, old man."

Mickey walked Goldstein across the hall into their suite and sat down while Goldstein viewed the painting, taking only a few minutes before turning around and saying, "What's next?"

Mickey said, "I'll take you back to your suite, and then please write down your bid on a piece of paper, fold it and I'll pick it up shortly."

Goldstein nodded, shook hands with Paul, smiled and bowed slightly to Jennifer. Mickey took him back to his suite, then walked over and knocked on Chiusolo's door. He answered with a big smile. "I can't wait," he said. Mickey led him into their suite, followed by Franchetti. Chiusolo admired the painting from five feet away while Franchetti did his routine. After a few minutes Chiusolo sat down next to Mickey on the sofa. He said,

"Thanks again, bro. Like I told you earlier, Georgianne's gonna flip." He smiled at Paul. Then he turned and winked at Jennifer and ruffled his eyebrows for her. Jennifer laughed. After about 10 minutes Franchetti turned around and nodded. Chiusolo stood up immediately and said, "Great."

Mickey took him back across the hall and gave Chiusolo the same instructions he'd given Goldstein.

After 10 minutes, Mickey left the room and crossed to Goldstein's suite. He knocked and Goldstein opened the door, smiling, with a folded sheet of the hotel's stationery in his hand.

"Good luck," Mickey said, took it and pulled the door shut. He walked over to Chiusolo's suite and knocked. Chiusolo opened the door and handed Mickey a folded piece of paper, saying, "I'm not even gonna wait until her birthday to give it to her."

Mickey walked back into their suite and sat down on the sofa. He put both pieces of paper on the coffee table. Jennifer and Paul squeezed in on each side of him, peering at the two folded papers on the coffee table. Mickey waited for a moment, then unfolded Goldstein's bid: *$20 million.* He opened Chiusolo's: *$40 million.*

Paul stood up from the sofa and pumped a fist in the air. "Yes!" he said.

Jennifer glared at him.

Now Mickey could feel Jennifer's gaze boring in on him; he turned to meet it. "You're not going to, are you?" she said.

Mickey shook his head. "No, but I'm going to see if I can work Goldstein for a little more."

Paul said, "Mickey, Chiusolo's at 40 million bucks."

Jennifer said to Paul, "Am I really going to have to spend the rest of my life smacking you back in line?"

Paul shrugged and smiled. "Think how bored you'd be if you didn't, babe."

Mickey stood up and walked to the door. He stopped with his hand on the knob and turned back. "Any final comments?"

Paul said, "Man, it really is about Goldstein, isn't it?"

Mickey's cell phone rang. He looked at the screen: BUFFETT. Mickey had called him the night before and wasn't sure after the debacle with Bernoulli that Buffett would call back. Mickey walked over and sat down on one of the chairs across from the sofa.

"Hi, thanks for calling back."

"Sure. What's up?" Acting as if the whole Bernoulli thing never happened.

"First, I wanted to apologize for inconveniencing you in the *View of the Sea* process. We're going forward with the sale, despite what your man, Bernoulli, said the other day. I should let you know that I was told by a reliable source that Walter Goldstein paid off Bernoulli to sabotage our process."

"Who on earth told you that?"

"Walter Goldstein." Mickey didn't wait for a response, just kept going. "But that's not why I called. I had something else I wanted to ask you. When we first talked about *View of the Sea*, you mentioned to me that you own a van Gogh from the same period, *Women Mending Nets in the Dunes*, that you're looking to sell."

"Yes, I'm thinking of using Christie's."

"As I recall, you told me you thought they could sell it for $18 to $20 million, gross."

"That's right."

"So if a seller tells me 18 to 20, that means he's thinking he'd like to get 18, otherwise why not say 20 to 25, right?"

Buffett chuckled.

Mickey said, "So I'm thinking $18 million at auction, less Christie's 12% premium, that's $16 million net to you. I've got a friend who'd love to own that painting, and I think I could get you $16 million for it in a private sale. Would you be interested?"

"I assume you're representing this friend."

"No. I'm just doing him a favor. He's trying to buy *View of the Sea* but isn't going to make the cut. This would be a nice consolation prize for him."

"I'm not sure at $16 million, Mickey. You know how crazy things get in auctions. Christie's could wind up selling the darned thing for $25 million."

"How about $18 million and he flies out tomorrow to pick it up?"

Buffett thought for a moment. "I assume the man is legit or you wouldn't be asking me."

"It's John Chiusolo."

"I know who he is. Sure. Consider we've got a handshake."

"Great. Thanks. I'll tell John and I'll get back to you on the details." Mickey hung up.

Jennifer was beaming. "Close your eyes, honey," she said to Paul.

She stood up and walked across to where Mickey sat. She leaned over and cupped his face in her hands, nose to nose with him. "You've got soul, Mickey," she said. Then she kissed him; a soft, affectionate one, for a few seconds. When she pulled back she hovered there for another moment. She said, "I think in your world the word is '*mensch*.'" She kissed him again.

Mickey got up, walked across the hall and knocked on Goldstein's door. He made sure his face was blank when Goldstein opened it.

"We need to talk," Mickey said, walked past Goldstein and sat down on the sofa.

"Where are we?" Goldstein said.

"I can't quite believe it, but we have a tie. So I'm going to ask each of you to take your last and best shot." Mickey stood up. "No need to write anything down. Just tell me."

Goldstein looked flustered, as if he couldn't believe it, and yet was faced with a reality he couldn't ignore.

Mickey said, "So, do you want to stick where you are or bump your price?"

Goldstein walked over and grabbed the back of a chair, pressing his fingers into the cushion. He cleared his throat. "Very well. I'll go to 25, but that's my final offer."

Mickey said, "Okay," frowned and headed straight for the door. His fingers were tingling as he reached for the doorknob, hoping. He turned it and opened the door.

Goldstein called out, "Wait."

Mickey closed the door and turned back to look.

"Alright. $30 million."

Mickey wasn't sure, but he thought he detected perspiration on Goldstein's upper lip. He nodded, opened the door and crossed the hall into their suite. He smiled and said, "He went to 30."

Paul, who was standing, laughed and hunched over.

"Shush," Jennifer said.

Smiling, Mickey walked over to the table where he'd left his computer. He said to Jennifer, "Bring the painting and Goldstein's cell phone in a few minutes, please." He walked back to Goldstein's suite and knocked.

Goldstein's face was almost in a panic as he opened the door.

"Okay," Mickey said. "Let's do this."

Mickey walked over to the coffee table, opened the computer and logged into the hotel's wireless network. He opened a connection to the Internet bitcoin currency site and then swung the computer around so Goldstein could access it. He handed Goldstein an account number on a piece of paper. Goldstein sat down in front of the computer just as Jennifer walked in with the painting in the case. She slid it out and propped it up on the sofa next to Goldstein, then put his cell phone next to it. Goldstein typed into the computer, then turned it around for Mickey to see.

Goldstein said, "Hit SEND and the transfer of gold bitcoin currency will be made. Then check your account."

Mickey hit SEND, saw the transfer go out, logged out of Goldstein's account and logged into his own: $30 million in funds were there, untraceable.

He closed the computer and stood up. "We're done here. A pleasure doing business with you." He extended his hand and Goldstein shook it, then quickly slid the painting back into the case and headed for the door.

Jennifer said, "I'll escort you downstairs and take you wherever you want to go in the limo."

"That won't be necessary," Goldstein said and left without looking back.

Mickey walked out of Goldstein's suite and knocked on Chiusolo's door. He tried to keep his face neutral when he said, "Can we talk privately?"

"Oh, man, bro, I can see it in your face." Chiusolo motioned for Franchetti to leave and Mickey stepped inside and closed the door. "Don't do this to me. Not again," Chiusolo said.

"You lost."

Chiusolo didn't respond.

"But I do have something else I can offer you if you're interested. I'm going to send you a link to a photo of another van Gogh from the same period. It's called *Women Mending Nets in the Dunes*, and was painted in the same year with the same atmospherics as *View of the Sea*. Buffett owns it and was going to take it to Christie's to auction it, thinks it might go for as much as $25 million, but I convinced him to part with it for $18 million in a private sale. I told him you're the buyer and he says you've got a handshake at that number if you want it. You can fly out and pick it up tomorrow."

Chiusolo didn't respond for a moment, then whispered, "You're the best, bro. The best." Chiusolo grabbed Mickey's hand in both of his and shook it. Then he cleared his throat and said, "And Georgianne will love the fact that I bought it from Buffett."

"I'll set it up," Mickey said.

As Mickey turned to leave, Chiusolo said, "I've gotta know, what did Goldstein pay for *View of the Sea*?"

"Thirty million."

Chiusolo opened his mouth in surprise. "Bro, I don't get it."

Mickey said, "Let me put it this way. The van Gogh you're buying is real." He opened the door and left.

When Mickey walked back into their suite, Jennifer and Paul were standing near the door. "We could hear Chiusolo laughing over here," Paul said. "What was that all about?"

Mickey told them.

Paul said, "Man, was that smart? You said yourself the guy has a big mouth. Inside of a week it'll be all over the art world that Goldstein paid $30 million for a fake van Gogh."

Mickey just shook his head.

"Honey, sometimes you're such a dufus," Jennifer said. "That's exactly the point. Goldstein will be a laughingstock, ruined."

As soon as they returned to Jennifer's apartment, Paul headed straight for the kitchen. "Champagne!" he yelled.

"It's not even noon," Mickey said.

"When're you gonna lighten up?" Paul called over his shoulder.

Paul opened the first bottle and they all toasted, then Mickey sat down on the sofa, opened his computer and started transferring the split: 20% to Bouchard and 26.7% to each of Jennifer, Paul and himself.

Jennifer said, "I never expected a full share."

Mickey shrugged. "It's the only fair thing to do. Six million to Bouchard and $8 million for each of us."

Paul said, "I can't believe it, I just can't believe it, man. Eight million bucks."

"Believe it," Mickey said, smiling, now allowing himself to feel it for the first time.

It took Bouchard over an hour to return Mickey's phone call. When he did, and Mickey told him what happened, Bouchard kept saying "Incredible" over and over. "Just incredible." Then he started talking about another painting he could copy and Mickey laughed, thanked him again and signed off. They were well into their third bottle of champagne when Holden phoned Mickey.

"I think it's only fair to tell you that we're hearing from a credible source that Moravian White has left the city, and maybe even the country."

Mickey just listened, not sure he should believe it.

Holden continued. "Our resources are always strained, so under the circumstances I'm pulling the team from your ex-wife's apartment. And by the way, let me give you some friendly advice."

Mickey wanted to tell Holden he didn't think anything that came out of his mouth was friendly, but he held his tongue.

"Check in with your parole officer, let him know where you're staying or you might find yourself back in jail."

Mickey hung up, hoping it was the last time he'd ever hear from Charlie Holden.

———◆———

Mickey had called Rachel twice and not heard back from her. It was a week after they sold Goldstein the painting when Rachel finally called him back, in tears.

"It turns out you were right about Walter," she said.

"I don't recall ever telling you my opinion of Walter."

"Oh, Mickey, you wore it on your sleeve. You're characteristically reserved, as you were whenever Walter's name came up, but I could tell you thought he was a fraud."

Mickey waited, his heart starting to pump harder, yet telling himself to let her go on in her own time.

"Three days ago when I came home from lunch with Rebecca, I noticed a number of Walter's things were gone. I checked the closets, but all his suits were still there, so I didn't think anything of it, just believed he'd suddenly gone to Europe again on another art buying trip and would call. After three days of calling his cell phone and his gallery, nothing. Until a half hour ago, when Walter finally phoned me." She paused, and he could hear her crying, then blowing her nose. She came back. "He said he lost every nickel of my money that he invested in his gallery and art. I pleaded with him to explain how that could possibly happen, but all he said was he lost it on a bad transaction, and he's going to have to close the gallery in New York and return to Europe. He's breaking off our engagement."

She started crying again.

"I'm coming over," Mickey said.

"Oh, Mickey, I'm so ashamed. You were always my rock. And now without you, I just don't know what to do. I feel like I'm just such a worthless, ridiculous fool."

"Stop it," Mickey said. "I'm coming over."

Mickey hung up and got ready to go out. Paul saw him walking toward the door with his topcoat on and said, "What's up?"

"I'm going over to Rachel's. Goldstein left her, big surprise. He said he'd done a bad deal, lost all her money and is folding up his tent here in New York, going back to Europe. He's broken it off with her."

Paul smiled. "Congratulations. But you're not serious about going over there now, are you?"

"Of course."

"That nut, Moravian White, might still be out there. And if he is, he's probably still watching Rachel's apartment building. You show up, he goes wacko again with that semi-automatic and maybe this time he doesn't miss."

Mickey said, "Rachel is flat-out at rock bottom. I've never heard her like this. She needs me. I'm going."

Mickey took a cab to Park Avenue and 57th Street, got out and walked up to Rachel's apartment building at 63rd Street. The night was brisk, characteristic for mid-November in New York. It was early evening, not many cabs going north but lots of them heading south, taking New Yorkers from early dinners to the Theater District. The wind whipped up, Mickey marveling that New York still kept Park Avenue so clean, no papers swirling up in the wind. At least some things hadn't changed much in the last 100 years. He smiled, feeling a part of New York again, the city and world he loved. As he approached 63rd Street, he started feeling lightness in his arms and legs from anticipation, then got a spurt of adrenaline.

He remembered Paul's warning, then told himself, *Nothing's going to happen. White's not here.*

He was across 63rd Street now, no more than 15 feet from the familiar brass-canopied entrance to 575 Park, the place he'd called home for so long, when a man stepped out from a doorway near the corner of 64th Street and started walking toward him. He wore a dark hoodie with the hood pulled up so Mickey couldn't see his face, but he was walking fast, with intent. Mickey felt a rise of alarm at about the same time the man pulled one hand out of his pocket and raised his arm toward Mickey.

He's got a gun! It's White! Mickey collapsed to the ground just as White fired his pistol at him. Then White aimed up to Mickey's left and Mickey saw a flash and heard the crack of a gun right above him, once, twice, three times. White went over backward like he'd been slammed in the chest by a truck, then down on the sidewalk. Mickey got to his knees, his ears ringing from the gunshots. Someone grabbed him from behind by the collar and pulled him to his feet.

"Come on!" he barked into his face. It was Paul. "I may not be fit for cop work anymore, but I can still shoot. Let's get the hell out of here, man."

———◇———

After shoving Mickey into a cab and climbing in after him, Paul kept a close eye on him. Mickey didn't say a word in the first five minutes of the ride toward Jennifer's apartment, just stared straight ahead out the windshield, his eyes not even showing that lazy blink he did when he was thinking. Finally he turned to Paul and said, "Thanks. That's twice you've saved me."

Paul said to him, "You didn't think I was gonna let you go over there alone, did you?"

He thought he saw Mickey try to smile, but his face was so tense that his lips just twitched. Mickey said, "Have you ever been shot at before?"

"When I was a cop, but never twice in two weeks by the same guy."

Mickey turned and stared straight ahead again.

Paul got Mickey upstairs to Jennifer's apartment and sat him down at the kitchen table, made tea for both of them. Jennifer was still out at an Angels function.

After a few sips of tea, Mickey said, "You think he's dead?"

"Three shots in the chest with a .38 from 20 feet away. I don't think you'll be seeing Moravian White again."

Mickey nodded. After a moment he said, "Maybe there'll be something about it on the news later, or in the paper tomorrow."

Mickey slept late the next morning and was awakened by the sound of his phone ringing. It was Holden.

"You still in one piece?"

"What do you mean?"

"Stop me if you've already heard this one. Moravian White was shot dead in front of your ex-wife's apartment building last night. There was a Glock semi-automatic lying on the street next to him with one round fired. I guess he missed you." He paused, maybe waiting for a response. When Mickey didn't say anything, Holden went on. "Sorry I gave you bad information about White skipping town."

Mickey said, "I'm just glad that neither Rachel nor I will ever have to worry about him anymore."

"I understand that knucklehead ex-con friend of yours is also an ex-cop. He didn't by any chance own a snub-nosed Smith & Wesson .38 with the serial number filed off, did he?"

"Is this conversation going anywhere?"

Holden paused for a moment, then said, "Stay out of trouble," and hung up.

Two weeks later Mickey sat in the Park Avenue co-op, a glass of Bordeaux in his hand, *La Bohème* playing on the stereo and Rachel at his side on the sofa. Rachel turned to him and said, "Oh my God, look at the time."

"It's 5:35."

Rachel jumped up from the sofa. "I need to get the food ready."

"It's only Hector and Maria, Paul and Jennifer. Just cocktails, and then we're going out."

Rachel headed for the kitchen and called over her shoulder, "They'll be here at six. I can't still be throwing things onto serving platters as they walk in the door."

Mickey smiled. Before he went away to Yankton, Rachel would have had cocktails and hors d'oeuvres catered. Now she thought they were on a budget again, like when they were newlyweds. And in a way they were; $8 million wasn't pocket change, but in today's world they could live comfortably but not extravagantly on it over the rest of their lives. Except for living in a Park Avenue apartment, it was like the old days. Even his closets were almost empty, only four suits where he used to keep dozens—as had Goldstein, until Rachel donated them to the thrift shop at the temple.

Mickey put down his glass of wine, stood up and walked into the kitchen to help her. Cheese and crackers, some guacamole and corn chips in honor of Hector and Maria, and chopped liver from the deli around the corner with bagel chips. He figured Paul would splurge on a good bottle of burgundy or two. After cocktails they'd all go to the Cuban restaurant that Hector had recommended on Avenue A. Mickey smiled, seeing Rachel from behind as she stood at the refrigerator. She was still a fine looking woman. They'd had a great life together. Now they had a wonderful future in front of them, and there was nothing better in the world than being here at home with her again.

After they finished cocktails—Paul had in fact brought two excellent bottles of Pierre Bourée Charmes-Chambertin, 1990—Rachel was giving Jennifer and Maria a tour of the apartment before they all went out to dinner. Hector turned to Mickey and said, "You ever hear anything more about Goldstein?"

"Only what Rachel told me."

Paul said, "Out of curiosity I did go down to Soho and saw that his gallery is closed and all the walls are empty. I guess we really did wreck the guy."

Mickey smiled and shrugged. "I don't know."

Paul said, "The guy pays us $30 million for a bogus painting, and after that he closes his gallery, breaks off his engagement and leaves New York with his tail between his legs. What more do you want?"

Mickey said, "You're the one who showed me your cop friend's research. Goldstein's actions are consistent with his modus operandi. He was in New York for about five years, worked his game until he found an easy mark in Rachel, scammed her for her money and took off to set up someplace else and do it all over again."

Hector was smiling and nodding his head.

Paul said, "How could he survive shoveling 30 million bucks down the drain?"

Mickey said, "You never know. Maybe all along he did have a big-ticket buyer waiting behind him and did his wholesale-to-retail markup, put $30 million more in profit in his pocket. And some Arab prince has a $60 million phony van Gogh hanging in his palace."

Paul said, "That would sure suck, man."

Mickey said, "There's an old adage on Wall Street: 'Don't look into the other guy's pocket.' I'm happy with how things turned out for us. Maybe I shouldn't care if we didn't ruin Goldstein."

Hector smiled and said, "Yeah, but you do care, don't you?"

"Hell yes."

Paul said, "You gonna just leave it like that, not knowing for sure?"

"Hell no."

AUTHOR'S NOTE

Vincent van Gogh's 1882 oil painting, *View of the Sea at Scheveningen,* was stolen from the Van Gogh Museum in Amsterdam on December 7, 2002, and has never been recovered. The FBI estimated the painting's value at $15 million. Authorities believe the thieves may have sold the painting to a wealthy art collector who retains it in his private collection to this day.

ABOUT THE AUTHOR

 David Lender is a former investment banker who spent 25 years on Wall Street. After earning his MBA at Northwestern University's Kellogg School of Management, he went on to work in mergers and acquisitions for Merrill Lynch, Rothschild, and Bank of America. His first three novels—*Trojan Horse, The Gravy Train* and *Bull Street*—turned him into an e-book sensation. He lives in northern New Jersey with his family and a pitbull named Styles. More background on David and his writing can be found at www.davidlender.net.